PRAISE FOR *JUMP CUT*
FROM **SEVEN (THE SERIES)**

"Readers will thoroughly enjoy *Jump Cut* on its own or as part of this unique new series. Highly Recommended." —*CM Magazine*

"[An] entertaining story with a heart of gold." —*Kirkus Reviews*

"The dialogue is very amusing, sharp and revealing of character..." —*Resource Links*

PRAISE FOR *CODA*
FROM **THE SEVEN SEQUELS**

"This clever spy adventure features a likable hero and bursts with enough film references to satisfy all but the most hard-core movie buffs." —*Kirkus Reviews*

"A fun read with interesting characters and a quirky plotline." —*CM Magazine*

"A good choice for anyone who likes mystery and action books." —*Canadian Teacher Magazine*

D1108759

SPEED

TED STAUNTON

ORCA BOOK PUBLISHERS

Copyright © 2016 Ted Staunton

All rights reserved. No part of this publication may be reproduced
or transmitted in any form or by any means, electronic or mechanical, including
photocopying, recording or by any information storage and retrieval system now
known or to be invented, without permission in writing from the publisher.

Library and Archives Canada Cataloguing in Publication

Staunton, Ted, 1956–, author
Speed / Ted Staunton.
(The seven prequels)

Issued in print and electronic formats.
ISBN 978-1-4598-1161-4 (paperback).—ISBN 978-1-4598-1162-1 (pdf).—
ISBN 978-1-4598-1163-8 (epub)

I. Title.
PS8587.T334S7 2016   jc813'.54   C2016-900489-9
                            C2016-900490-2

First published in the United States, 2016
Library of Congress Control Number: 2016933643

Summary: In this middle-grade novel, Spencer ends up
in the middle of a War of 1812 reenactment.

*Orca Book Publishers is dedicated to preserving the environment and has
printed this book on Forest Stewardship Council® certified paper.*

Orca Book Publishers gratefully acknowledges the support for its publishing
programs provided by the following agencies: the Government of Canada
through the Canada Book Fund and the Canada Council for the Arts,
and the Province of British Columbia through the BC Arts Council
and the Book Publishing Tax Credit.

Design by Teresa Bubela
Cover photography by iStock.com
Author photo by Margaret Heenan

ORCA BOOK PUBLISHERS
www.orcabook.com

Printed and bound in Canada.

19 18 17 16 • 4 3 2 1

In loving memory of my mom,
who made me wear shorts

ONE

When I rule the world my first law will be that skinny—I mean, *slim*—guys like me never have to wear dumb giant cargo shorts, even if their parents tell them to. My second law will be that we can take our cell phones anywhere.

See, if my parents, Deb and Jer, had just let me bring my new phone on this trip, I wouldn't have had to hide it in these stupid monster shorts to sneak it along. And if they had let me wear regular jeans with regular pockets, I would have known right away that it was gone when I lost it.

So it's practically not even my fault that it's gone—except it is.

I notice my phone is missing right after we finish setting up the tents, one for Grandpa and one for me and my younger brother, Bunny. Grandpa and Bunny are off getting wood for tonight's campfire. I'm lugging our stuff from Grandpa's Jeep into the tents when I stop to check my phone battery. I'm worried about power sources out here in the wild. Okay, it's not the wild. It's the campground of Queenston Provincial Park, but it might as well be the wild: I hate camping. Anyway, I go to check my phone and it's not there.

Oh. No. My phone is *brand new*. I do a total speed search everywhere: shorts, tents, the Jeep. Nothing. I do it all again. Still nothing. I say a whole bunch of words I'm not supposed to know. They don't help. Panting, I duck into Grandpa's tent and look again. All I see is a book crammed in the top of Grandpa's pack: *Billion-Dollar Brain*. It's not about me, that's for sure. As I fight my panic, I hear Bun and Grandpa coming back. Oh no, no, no. I run out, grab sleeping bags and foam pads and pitch them into the tents. Behind me I hear the clatter of falling wood. I turn, trying to look like a happy camper. I'm sweating, and it's not even very hot.

"Good going, Bernard." Grandpa always calls Bunny by his real name. He unzips his RCAF shell, pushes up his fishing hat and wipes his forehead. Usually he wears a beret, but maybe a beret's not summer camp enough. "Tents shipshape, Spencer?"

"Almost."

Grandpa nods. "Okay, men, here's the plan. We'll walk the boundaries of where you can roam solo, then I'll have a little lie-down, and then we'll hunt up some excitement." Grandpa checks his big flier's watch. "Excellent, it's just one thirty. C'mon with me. Now, pay attention, boys. I'm going to trust you both and I want you to have fun, but this is not a normal weekend at the park. There'll be surprises."

"Surprises like a birthday party?" Bun asks.

I don't hear the answer. Losing my phone is surprise enough for me. As Grandpa leads us across the campground I whisper to Bunny, "There's a problem."

"What about?" he whispers back.

"I lost my phone. Where did you last see it?"

"In your hand."

"But where was that?"

"Right there." Bun points. At my hand.

"I know where my hand is, Bun Man. But where was I when you saw my phone?"

He thinks about this as Grandpa points out how far we can go. "Ice cream," Bunny says.

"We just had some, Bernard," Grandpa says over his shoulder.

I feel a cool scoop of hope. They're both right: we stopped at an ice-cream place just outside the park gates. I remember getting out my phone when Grandpa hit the washroom. Bun and I were sitting at a picnic table and I shoved the phone under my leg when Grandpa came back sooner than I expected. Then Bun and I went to the Jeep while he got extra napkins for the cones.

Now Grandpa is saying, "True gen, boys: watch for poison ivy. The old P.I. will get you every time, and the woods will be full of it."

Another reason not to wear dumb shorts, I think. Grandpa's not wearing shorts. He calls his tan pants *chinos*. Whatever. I'm not going there again now. There's something else I have to do. As Grandpa ducks into his tent for a snooze I grab Bunny. "I'm going back to get my phone. I'll be fast. If Grandpa wakes up, don't tell him, okay? Tell him I've gone exploring. He'll like that. See you later, Bun Man." I take off for the road we came in on.

TWO

The gates are farther away than I thought. It doesn't matter. Remembering how I argued with Deb and Jer about bringing my phone keeps me going.

Jer had said, *If you lost it in the woods, you'd never find it.* Then Deb said, *Remember the rule? Lose it and you're not getting another. That thing cost a fortune. You don't need a phone in a campground.*

Oh yes you do. The only thing more boring than camping is TV golf. I need the games on my phone to survive. Games are the most important part of a good phone, except for a place to charge it, which I will find somewhere in this stupid park after I get my phone. I didn't say that though, because Grandpa had chimed in with *Camping is about escaping cell phones, Spencer.*

But what if there's an emergency?

That's what grandpas are for. I'll have mine in the Jeep. Turned off.

Case closed, said Deb.

Well, this is one emergency Grandpa can't deal with. What makes it worse is, I was really, truly, only going to play games at bedtime or when Grandpa was napping—for a reward, like. I figured I'd deserve it.

See, Jer had given me a pep talk. *This trip means a lot to your Grandpa D. He wants to take each of his grandsons somewhere, bond with you. Bernie would love to do the same thing.* Bernie is Jer's dad, my other grandpa. He and Estelle live out west on Salt Spring Island. Grandpa D is Deb's dad, David McLean. *It's just a weekend,* Jer went on. *Promise to try to be a happy camper, okay? Just go with the flow, give it a chance, and*

I bet you'll have fun. And Grandpa D will love it. He'll be proud of you.

That's true. Grandpa knows I suck at outdoors stuff, and I know that bugs him. Luckily, when we go to his cottage, Bun and our cousins take up the slack for me while I read comics under the deck. I take up the slack for Bun when Grandpa starts giving us advice. Deb calls that Grandpa's *lecture mode.* She should know—she's a prof at York U, and if that's what university is like, I think I'll skip it.

I puff up to the SofteeSlurp ice-cream stand, my glasses smeared with sweat. There's no phone where we sat. A teenager is bagging trash and wiping tables. I hurry over. "Did anyone turn in a phone?"

He shakes his head. "No, but I saw some dude pick one up from over there, maybe an hour ago." He points to the table we were at.

How long ago were we here? If I had my phone, I'd know. "Was the phone yellow?" I ask. He shrugs. His SofteeSlurp shirt has a rainbow of stains.

Maybe he doesn't notice colors. I try again. "What did he look like?"

He shrugs again. "Tall. He had a blue coat and a weird hat. The hat's why I remember. Light pants, maybe white."

Maybe he does notice colors. "Did you see where he went?"

"Probably into the park." He hefts a trash bag and walks away.

I am mega-doomed. I head back into the park myself, kicking at gravel on the road. Somewhere in here is a tall guy in a blue jacket, a funny hat and white pants who stole my phone. How am I going to find him? What will I do if I *do* find him? Maybe Bun and I could team up. I imagine Bun karate-kicking him into a batch of poison ivy while I swoop down from the trees to catch my phone as it goes sailing out of the guy's greedy, hairy hand. I wish. It ain't gonna happen, as Jer would say.

Instead, what if, when we get home, I just say I left it in the living room? I could even ask where it is. How could it be my fault if no one can find it? Bun wouldn't rat me out.

Problem is, I'm a bad liar. Deb, especially, can tell. *A teacher's heard a million excuses,* she always says to me if I try something. Besides, even if I got away with it, having a guilty secret might be worse than having Deb and Jer go hyperballistic for a week, say, and then getting over it. And either way, I'd never get a phone again.

I'm still thinking this over when I hear strange thumping noises. I look up and find I've got a new problem—I don't know where I am. Have I taken a wrong turn? This is not what I need right now. The thumping is coming from behind a line of trees I don't remember. Something's moving back there. I shove my glasses up and jog over. A voice barks something. I hear clattering and scraping and then I'm peering through the leaves at a line of men holding rifles. They're all pointed at me.

"Fire!" There's a rolling clap of thunder, and the world rips in half. Dragon flames belch from the rifle barrels. I think I yell as I jump back, and then I'm down. A gray-white cloud swallows me, and the world goes silent. I'm wrapped in cotton; I don't even feel my wounds. Is this what dying is like? If it is, dying smells like the firecrackers Grandpa has for us at the cottage on the long weekend. Then the men with guns burst sound-lessly through the cloud, mouths open, stabbing the air in front of them with bayonets as they run past me. I tuck into a ball and feel their boots thud past.

The ground stops shaking. I open my eyes. I can see—my glasses have made it to heaven with me. If that's where I am. What I'm seeing through the cloud is my feet, lying on a thick electrical cable snaking along the ground, inches from a patch of poison ivy. I wiggle my toes. They work. So do my fingers. I pat my body for bullet holes. I don't feel any. There's no blood on my hands either. Maybe I'm alive. I sit up. Now my ears are ringing, and I hear a voice, faintly, from some-where past the smoke, which is drifting away.

I look up. Back where the men fired their rifles at me three people are standing. Grandpa would call them kids, but they're way older than me, and I'm finishing grade seven. They're university age maybe. They've got some kind of camera and some other equipment. One of them is waving this way.

I look behind me. The men have stopped running, just past the trees. They're taking the bayonets off their rifles and beginning to stroll back. One is lighting a cigarette. A couple more are checking their cell phones. I see now they're all in old-fashioned soldier uniforms that I recognize from school. The War of 1812. And guess what? Their uniforms are white pants, blue coats and tall funny hats.

THREE

The ringing in my ears is pretty much gone by the time the soldiers get to me. I'm standing up, trying to look as if I should be here.

"That go okay?" one of them asks me. He's carrying a sword instead of a rifle.

"Oh. Yeah. Great."

"You could hear my orders?"

"I sure heard the 'fire' part." I nod. I hate it when I don't know what's going on.

"Good. Listen," says the man, "will you take this back for me? I've really gotta hit the can, and I sure won't need it there." He chuckles as he unclips a little microphone from the standup collar of his blue coat and fishes out a wire and battery pack. "A good charge always does this to me." He hands me the stuff. "Thanks."

"But—" I start to say. The man is already trotting away, hanging on to his sword. Other guys in blue coats are almost at the camera. I hustle after them, wishing Bun was here. Whatever's going on, if one of them has my phone, I don't want to lose him too.

The three people at the camera, two guys and a girl, are packing equipment into a little metal suitcase. I hand the baby microphone and battery pack to one of them. "Cool," he says without looking up. He checks a switch on the battery and stows it in a foam-lined box. "Grab the other two from those guys." A couple more 1812 soldiers are standing nearby, taking off their microphones. They've put their rifles and tall black hats on the ground. I walk over, and that's when I stop breathing for real. On top of one guy's hat is my cell phone. I mean, I think it's my phone. It looks exactly like it, and this soldier is in the right clothes. It *has* to be my cell phone. I think.

How can I find out? *Hey, did you steal that phone?* will probably not work. Should I just grab the phone and take off? Um, no. I'm a slow runner, and this guy has a gun and a bayonet. Bunny could probably do it, but not me. Besides, what if it's not my phone? Grandpa, Deb and Jer are going to be even madder if I lose my phone *and* go to jail for stealing someone else's.

What if I knock over his hat, pick up the phone to help and check the contacts before I give it back? Sure, and maybe I'll also sprinkle myself with magic fairy dust to be invisible. I'm out of time for deciding. I'm asking for the microphones as they unclip their battery packs. I can't take my eyes off the phone. My phone. Maybe. "Nice phone," I hear myself say. Maybe I can ask to look at it.

"Thanks," says the guy, handing me his mic and battery. "Just got it."

Just got it. Now the other soldier is handing me his stuff. My hands are full. How can I ask to see the phone now? I ask, "Have you, uh, been to the SofteeSlurp place?"

The soldier is tugging at these white belts that cross on his chest. He gives me a sharp look. I freeze. Does he know I know? Then he laughs and points to a pink stain on the belt. "Good noticing. Yeah, don't get the Cherry Bubble Gum. I'll have to clean this when we get back to camp. Hope Luther doesn't see it first. How farb would an ice-cream stain be?"

The other guy says, "How farb is a cell phone?"

"Geez! Right."

Farb? *Farb?* They laugh as the first soldier shrugs the belt into place. He stuffs the phone into his pocket before I can do anything.

"Mics, please!" It's the guy packing the foam-lined box. I run to hand them in. I have to follow that soldier. As I turn away, the movie guy says,

"You with the Yanks?" He doesn't wait for an answer. "Good. We're all going the same way." He has glasses, like me, and cargo shorts, except he's chubby so his legs don't look like twigs. His T-shirt reads *NIAGARA COLLEGE,* but stretched a little. My T-shirt says *ELO* and is not stretched at all.

"Could you carry that?" He nods at a gym bag with electrical cords sticking out.

"Sure," I say. This is my first break. Now I can follow the soldier without being noticed.

"Come on, Mark," the other movie guy is calling. He's got the camera. The girl has two backpacks. Mark grabs the metal suitcase and a tripod thing with a long arm attached. We start after the soldiers.

"What's next on the sked?" says the other movie guy. He's got on a ballcap and cool sunglasses.

The girl says, "The encampment, Basil. Should be lots of good stuff. Battle and cow tomorrow, then linking shots. Too bad Stef can't be here this aft. The light's so good."

"She's gotta work," Basil says. "She'll be here tonight."

"I know," the girl says. "Just saying." She's tall and pale. Her hair is short and dark. She looks at me. "Hi, I'm Tracey. Are you a new helper? Who are you with?"

"Um, David McLean." I don't know what else to say.

"I know that name, but I don't think I've seen you before. Is this your first?"

"First what?"

"First reenactment," Tracey says. "What role does David McLean do?"

"Mostly he's my grandpa. We're, like, camping, and he said there'd be a surprise."

"Oh!" she says. "I bet the surprise is all this." She nods at the soldiers up ahead. "There's a War of 1812 reenactment here this weekend, people camping and doing things as if it's 1812. They'll have a pretend battle too—tomorrow. It's a big hobby."

"Gee," I say. What else can I say? Adults are weird? I said before the only thing more boring than camping is TV golf. Check that. I'd forgotten about the War of 1812, which is more boring than the two put together. The only thing more boring than *it* would be healthy snacks. But I've promised to be a happy camper and I've got more important things to worry about, so I also say, "Neat."

Tracey nods as if it is quite cool. "I thought maybe your grandpa was a reenactor. My grandmother is, and me too sometimes. I've been to a million of these. That's how we got the idea for the movie."

I want to ask if the movie is for Hollywood, but before I can, we step into a time warp. Spread out in front of me is a pioneer camp. There are old-time white tents and two log buildings. Horses pull a wagon. People in old-fashioned clothes are tending fires and carrying tools and wooden buckets and putting up more tents. Somewhere, metal is clanging. Fiddle music floats in the air. There are soldiers in red coats, some in the blue I saw before, and people in Native costumes too. I remember from school that the red coats are British, the blue coats are American and that the Natives helped the British. And that the war was in 1812 and nobody can decide who won. What else do you need to know?

Now I see there are lots of people in normal clothes too, wandering through all this weirdness. That means Grandpa and Bun can't be too far away. Excellent. My soldier is still ahead of us. He said they were going to camp. When I find out where that is, I can go get Bun to help me and we'll think of something. I ask Tracey, "Where do the soldiers camp?"

She points. "The Americans are set up over there, and the British are next to them. See the old-fashioned tents? They're canvas, called wedge tents."

"Do you know where the regular campground is? I'm kind of lost."

"Oh, wow," she says, "sure." She pulls out a cell phone. "Do you want to call your grandpa? He might be worried."

I start to nod, then shake my head, fast. I almost forgot that Grandpa might not know I snuck away. He can be a pretty long napper. "I can't," I say. "His number is in my phone, and I lost that too."

"That sucks." Then she says, "Hey, I know where I heard your grandpa's name. My gram is an old friend or something. She said they're getting together this weekend. I bet she'll know where he is."

"But—"

"Come on, I've got to change anyway. Back in five," she says to the movie guys.

She leads me into the pioneers.

FOUR

Tracey is way older than me, but her gram looks a lot younger than Grandpa. Go figure that out. She's outside the front door of one of the log houses, working at a spinning wheel. Dark-red hair peeks out of her bonnet, and she's wearing an apron over a dress so long you can only see the toe of a black shoe as it pumps the spinning wheel. She stops and jumps up when Tracey says loudly that I'm David McLean's grandson.

"How delightful." She has a movie-star smile and an accent like the queen of England.

I remember to shake hands. "You must be Spencer and Bernard," she says.

"Just Spencer," I say. "Bunny, I mean, Bern—"

"David said you would be here this weekend," she says right over me. "I've looked forward to meeting you. I'm Irene Steele. Perhaps David has mentioned me. Where is he?"

Tracey explains loudly how I need to call Grandpa at the campground. I try to say I don't need to, that Grandpa's phone is probably turned off, but it's as if Irene Steele doesn't hear. "Of course," she says. She pulls a phone out of her apron pocket and keys something in. "Use mine. I've his number in." She passes me the phone. The name by the number she's pressed is Poochy. *Poochy*? "Wait, may I speak first?" she says. I give her back the phone. She pushes it in the side of her bonnet, waits, then says, "David? My dear, I'm here with young Spencer and Bernard and my granddaughter Tracey. When will you join us?…Well, he looks absolutely fine to me, my darling. Yes, Spencer and Bernard…Certainly you may speak with him. Hurry now. You'll spot me as always. Till then, my dear."

Irene Steele hands the phone to me. What's with the *and Bernard*? Bunny's not here. I'm wondering how deaf she is when I hear Grandpa say, "Spence?"

"Hi, Grandpa. I'm with Irene Steele."

"So I hear." Grandpa's voice is flat. That's a bad sign. I don't think I'm scoring high in the *proud of you* department yet. Sure enough, he says, "You want to tell me why you're with her, Spence, when I told you two to stay in the boundaries?"

All my schemes about keeping out of trouble go up in a puff of gun smoke. Like I said before, I'm a really bad liar. I say, "I know, Grandpa. It's just…well…" I shut my eyes and go for it. "I lost my phone, and I remembered I'd left it at the ice-cream place, and you'd already started your nap, and so I went there and it wasn't there, but the guy said a tall guy with a funny hat and blue coat and light pants took it, and I met these soldier guys with—"

"Spence." Grandpa cuts me off. "This is your new phone? The one you weren't supposed to bring?"

"Yeah, Grandpa." My eyes are still shut.

There's a silence, and then Grandpa says, "Spence, what color are my pants and jacket?" I picture his RCAF shell and chinos. "Ummm," I say, then "Oh," then "Ohhhhhhhh."

I have a thought I don't really want to have. It has to do with me maybe being dumber than a bag of hammers. I say, "Light pants and blue jacket?"

"Bingo. What's on my head?"

"Oh. Yeah. Right." I'm definitely dumber than a bag of hammers. I try to make up for it by saying, "Well, I don't think your fishing hat is funny though." Really, I do think Grandpa's fishing hat is funny—we all do—but like I said, I'm a bad liar.

"I've got your phone, Spence. I picked it up from the table right after you two went to the Jeep. Thought I'd see how long it would take for you to notice. Or 'fess up."

"Sorry, Grandpa."

"Apology accepted. Page turned. Glad you manned up. But you almost gave me a heart attack, buzzing off like that. I'm not going to ask whose idea it was, but judging by the spelling, Bernard wrote the note. *Back soon* is not spelled *B-A-K S-U-N*. Now, sit tight with Irene and her granddaughter till I get there. Clear?"

"Yeah, but—"

"Good. I'll be over soon. See you then." He clicks off.

My phone is found. I've confessed. Grandpa is not mega-angry. I should be happy, right? Relieved, at least.

I'm not. What did Grandpa mean by *whose idea*? And what *back soon* note? I have a bad feeling that now, instead of looking for my phone, I might be looking for Bunny.

FIVE

Is Bun with Grandpa, or does Grandpa think he's with me? It's hard to tell from what Grandpa said. Sometimes it's hard to tell things from what *Bunny* says. Bun is a year younger than me, and he's different. He's way better at sports and stuff than I am, but he has a lot of trouble with reading and writing, and that fools people. Really, he's smart, but he does things in odd ways and for his own reasons. I don't know what he's up to, but I can't rat Bun out if he's doing something now. After all, he didn't rat on me. All I do is say, "Thank you" to Irene Steele and give back her phone. "Grandpa said he'll be here soon."

"Pardon, my dear?"

I tell her again, louder.

"Ah. Yes. Splendid. Forgive my hearing, Spencer. I'm afraid I stood rather too close to some loud bangs as a young woman." She laughs as if this is a wonderful joke, then turns to Tracey. "Darling girl, why not show Spencer the encampment while he waits?"

"I've got to change first, Gram." To me she says, "Do you want to hang with the crew while they film around here? They could use the help."

"Sure," I say. I can also see if Bunny's around.

"We'll be back when your grandpa gets here," Tracey says. "You're doing the bell, right, Gram?"

"Certainly, dear."

Tracey disappears into the log cabin. I wait while Irene Steele tells tourists boring things about spinning wheels. They smile and nod as if they're interested, and a couple even take pictures.

I wish Tracey would hurry up. As the people leave, Irene Steele says to me, "I'm so looking forward to seeing your grandfather. It's been simply ages. I always tell him he retired too young."

I know Grandpa had a buying-and-selling business—*import/export*, he called it. He traveled a lot. Grandma McLean died when my mom and her sisters were just little, and Deb says Grandpa wants to spend time with us grandsons to make up for being away so much when our moms were young. "What work did you do?" I make sure to ask loudly.

"Oh, call it information services. Your grandfather was a real old pro, such fun. I learned so much from him."

"Uh-huh." I'm not so great at doing adult conversation. Irene Steele asks things about me. I tell her I'm twelve and going into grade eight. "And Bernard is such an interesting last name," she says. "Is it Flemish? Norman perhaps?"

"No," I say. "It's O'Toole."

"From where, dear boy?"

"From my dad, I guess." I'm totally confused, and I'm not even the deaf one.

Irene Steele looks a little puzzled herself. She says, "I meant, is your family name from Normandy? *Anbernard* sounds French."

"My last name is O'Toole." I say it extra loud.

"*O'Toole?* I could have sworn David said—"

"I have a brother named Bernard," I say even louder.

She laughs again, like this is the best joke ever. "That explains it."

"What kind of explosions did you stand too close to?" I ask her. Loudly.

More best joke ever. "Blame your grandfather, dear heart. There were always fireworks when he was around, ha-ha. But where is your brother?"

"Oh, around," I say. To change the topic, I ask, "Do you know what a farb is?"

Her eyebrows go up. "It's an expression for passing gas, dear boy." She looks around. "Did someone…"

"No, no!" I wave my hands to correct things, "Not fart, *farb*." I hear a laugh. Tracey steps out of the cabin. She's in a British redcoat uniform.

"Not tooting, Gram. *Farb* is reenactor slang for someone who doesn't take their role seriously enough—like, say, chewing bubble gum in uniform," she says to me.

"Or eating ice-cream cones and checking your cell phone."

"Right on." She laughs again. "Or wearing sun block."

"But where does it come from?"

"Nobody's sure. I was told it's *barf* with the letters switched. Anyway, it means super-fake. The opposite is hardcore. There's a guy with the Americans, Luther, who's super-hardcore. You'll see him. He's got orange sideburns out to here." She holds her hands out past her ears. "He can't stand farbiness. Girls in uniform? Don't get him started."

She puts on her tall black hat, shoulders her gun and grabs the backpacks. "See you, Gram.

We'll be back for the bell. C'mon," she says to me.

I pick up the bag of cables, and we start through the encampment. I wonder again if I should be looking for Bunny. He'll be easy to spot. He's wearing a baby-blue T-shirt with *BREAD* printed on it in fat, curvy white letters. My *ELO* shirt is red, and the lettering is different. Bun says he likes his shirt because it feels soft. He's not a looks kind of guy. We got the T-shirts from Jer, who said he got them a million years ago but never wanted to wear them. *How come you didn't get one that said* BAGELS? I asked him when I saw Bunny's. Bun and I like bagels better.

That's not what it meant, Jer said. *Bread and ELO were the names of bands I was embarrassed to like. They were really poppy.*

Then why did you get their shirts? ELO isn't even a word, I said.

Let's just say I was out of my mind, Jer said. He never did tell me what ELO stood for.

Anyway, I watch for *BREAD*, but I don't see it. There's too much to look at, and Tracey goes pretty fast. She really looks like a young soldier. I bet that's why she has short hair. "Is that a real rifle?" I ask her.

"Well, first, it's not a rifle. It's a flintlock musket. And it's a replica, not a real old one. I got it used for $500. But we load and fire them like the real thing—except we don't use musket balls, just blank charges." I begin to understand why I'm still alive. Tracey puts down the packs to salute a man with a face as red as his coat. He's got a swoopy hat with a plume, gold braid hanging off his shoulders, and a sword. He salutes back and stumps on.

"Officers," Tracey says. "Once you put on the uniform, you have to salute."

"Or you're a farb?" I say.

Tracey nods. "Or you're a farb."

SIX

For an older teenager, Tracey is really easy to talk to, so I ask her if the movie is for Hollywood. She laughs. "I wish. Nah, we're all students at Niagara College, and we have to make a ten-minute documentary film for our summer course."

"That shouldn't take very long," I say.

"You'd be surprised," she says. "We'll probably have to shoot hours of film to edit down to ten good minutes—and we have to string it with a through line." She starts to explain. It's hard to follow because in front of us Native people are posing for pictures, a roly-poly man in a tall hat and a too-small blue coat is playing a fiddle, and a tiny lady in a pioneer dress is leading a man in pioneer shirt and pants around by a rope tied to his belt. The man is stumbling as he follows her.

"What am I bid for this husband?" she shouts. "What is your offer for this alehouse of a man, this walking whiskey barrel?"

Tracey smiles. "Really, it was mostly wife auctions back then," she says. "But there were a few husbands too." I don't even ask.

At the far end of the encampment there's a red tent set up beside one of the park washrooms. *NC* is printed in white on its side, kind of like my *ELO*. A thick electrical cable is plugged into an outlet on the outside wall of the washroom. Basil, Mark and some others are there. We put down the equipment bags. They tease Tracey about her soldier makeover. She laughs.

"I'm on duty for a while. Spencer's going to help out. He can do slates. Don't forget to film the bell—I promised my gram. I'll see you there."

While I wonder what this bell stuff is, she slings her musket higher and goes off.

"C'mon, Spencer," Mark says, pointing. "Grab that clapperboard."

I pick up a mini version of the whiteboards in my school classroom. It's got a striped stick hinged to its top. Basil hefts a camera with a U-shaped shoulder rest. Mark has what might be a laptop slung over his shoulder, and he's carrying the tripod thingy again. There's a microphone on it, capped with black sponge. Another group with the same stuff heads off. "Let's go," Mark says. He checks a list he's written on his arm. "Blacksmith first."

I follow Mark and Basil back into the encampment. A reenactor has a fire going in a pit, with a bellows rigged up to blow on it. I know what the bellows is because Grandpa has a mini one for the cottage fireplace. The reenactor is holding something red-hot with a long pair of tongs, bashing it on an anvil as people watch.

Mark and Basil set up fast. Mark plants the microphone and aims it over the crowd. He flips open the laptop thing and pulls on headphones. Basil puts down the camera, takes the clapperboard from me and scribbles *A 3 / 1* on it with a marker. "Stand by the blacksmith and face me," he orders. "Know what to do?"

I'm not sure, but I nod. Basil perches his sunglasses on his cap brim and shoulders the camera. I hustle over by the blacksmith and turn to face him, holding the board in front of me. I see there's a microphone attached to the camera too. Right now I'm more interested in the sparks flying at me from the anvil.

"Sound," Basil says to Mark. "Speed," Mark says back. Basil points the camera at me. "Mark it," he calls. I find I do know what to do. Maybe I've seen it on TV or something. I swing up the striped stick and clap it down on the board, then get out of the way.

Basil films a few minutes, then says, "Cut" to Mark. We move on. After two or three stops we get to a crowd around a platform. The roly-poly fiddler is playing right beside it. Next to him is a bluecoat officer with only one arm. He makes up for it with the biggest mustache I've ever seen. On the platform, a tourist is sitting on a chair. He's wearing a straw hat and has an old-fashioned coat jammed over his shorts and shirt. I now know that's farb. Above him on a pole is a wooden bucket filled with water, with a rope holding it back from tipping. The rope runs over and down, across the middle of a target painted on a big board that leans against a hay bale. A lady tourist is giggling as she tries to throw a hatchet at the rope. She misses big-time, and the hatchet lands in the hay. Everyone laughs. Someone else tries and misses. Everyone laughs again. "Let's get this," says Basil.

We set up again. By now I'm marking the clapperboard myself. This one is *A 7 / 1* for camera A, shot 7, take 1. Feeling like a pro, I stand by the platform with the clapperboard and mark the shot. Basil films while three more laughing tourists try to cut the rope with hatchet throws. He swivels back and forth between the platform and the throwers. He's told me that's called panning. Wait till I tell Bunny.

Now a big reenactor dressed like a farmer climbs up on the platform and helps the tourist down. Everybody claps. "I'll have a go," he cries. "There's none here can throw for tuppence. Bring on your best five." He plunks himself in the chair. More people make lame throws. "I'm drier than McGregor's tavern," calls the man on the chair, over the fiddle music. Everyone laughs again. As they do, the red-faced officer Tracey saluted stomps up.

"You were never dry in my regiment," he roars. "More tipple for the company drunkard!" He draws his sword and heads for the rope. Before he can cut it, the farmer jumps up.

"But wait! I've sat my five. Let's give another honest man a chance." Everyone laughs as he jumps down from the platform. Right beside me.

"Wanna help?" he whispers to me. "It's just buildup. Nobody can ever hit the rope. After you, I'll go back up, and Bob will cut it on me. I always get the splash."

Everyone's watching, including the camera. The reenactor winks. The fiddler winks. "Big cheer, guaranteed." If Bun were here, he'd be up in the chair by now. Grandpa would like that.

"Sure," I say. I step up. There *is* a big cheer, and then, before I know it, I'm in the coat and hat and on the chair.

The coat is too big, and the hat keeps slipping down over my glasses. I'm thinking they probably make a great combo with my cargo shorts. Everyone laughs as someone throws the hatchet and misses the rope. I wonder how skinny my legs are going to look in the movie. Can they be computer enhanced? I hear another laugh. Three more to go. I look over at Mark. He points at me and pretends to lift a hat off his own head. I get it. I take off the hat at the exact instant everyone shouts. Then the water hits me.

"Cut," Basil calls.

SEVEN

In case you're wondering, wet giant cargo shorts are even stupider than dry giant cargo shorts. Everyone is clapping and cheering as I slop down off the platform. "I'm sorry," says the big reenactor. "That's never happened before."

My glasses are so water streaked, I can't tell if he's really sorry, never mind see who splashed me. I wonder if it was that Luther guy. Maybe he thought cargo shorts were too farb.

I drip my way over to Mark. He's definitely grinning. "That's a keeper," he says.

"Thanks a bunch for the hat tip," I say, forgetting to be shy.

"Don't worry about it, Spencer." Basil comes up with the camera. "Movie baptism. You can shoot the next scene for us."

That helps. I wipe my glasses on my *ELO* shirt, which the jacket kept mostly dry. We take everything over to the log cabin, where more people are gathering. Irene Steele is bellowing, "Who knows the story of Laura Secord?" Her voice is like a British foghorn. A few yards away a cow is grazing, ignoring it all.

This time we set up differently. Basil fiddles with the camera, then shows me how to work it. He helps me settle the saddle onto my shoulder. "I'll stand beside Irene and do the slate," he says. "Cue Mark for sound, then focus on the clapperboard. When it's right, tell me to mark it and start rolling."

I nod. I want to get started. Forget 1812, forget camping, forget wet shorts even—this part is neat.

I'm not just some farb tourist. I'm helping make a movie with tech gear even cooler than my new phone. Bun's never done this. I bet *Grandpa's* never done this, and he's done almost everything. I ignore how heavy the camera is and how I look as if I have totally peed my shorts and peer into the viewfinder. The camera is out of focus, and I can't seem to get it right. "Try with your glasses off," Mark suggests. I shove them up and get my eye right in there. I wish I was wearing a ballcap I could turn backward.

I still can't get the focus. I put my glasses back on. Before I try again, I notice I've been pushing the wrong button. I don't mention that. "Got it," I say. Basil and the board swim into view. I spread my feet to brace myself. "Sound," I say to Mark. I hear him clicking buttons.

"Speed," he says back. That means the sound is recording. I get *A 8 / 1* in the middle of the frame. I press the Rec button on the camera's hand grip. "Mark it!"

The clapper cracks down on the board, Basil steps aside, and I'm filming a movie.

Actually, I'm filming Irene Steele. "…Laura Secord," she's booming. "She and her husband, James, lived in a cabin much like this in 1812. When James was wounded in the battle of Queenston Heights, Laura rescued him. Then in 1813 the Americans took over her house, and Laura heard them planning to attack the British garrison at Beaver Dam.

"James was still too weak to help, so Laura had to warn the British herself. She set off through the fields and woods to avoid the main road, leading her cow as if it had strayed."

Irene Steele points. I try to pan smoothly to the cow, but I wobble, which makes me say a couple of those words I'm not supposed to know. Saying them makes me remember there's a microphone attached to the camera. Remembering that makes me say the words again.

I shut up and find the cow. Apart from a tail swish, it couldn't care less. Two of the people behind the cow are more interesting anyway. One is a bluecoat reenactor with gigantic orange sideburns out to here and down to his chin. It has to be that Luther guy. Beside him is Grandpa. He's traded in his fishing hat for his beret.

Irene Steele goes on. "Laura walked twenty miles, some say barefoot, crossed Twelve Mile Creek on a fallen log and got to a Native camp to deliver her warning. Two days later the Americans walked into an ambush. Nearly five hundred surrendered to a much smaller British force." Luther is grimly shaking his sideburns, probably still mad about the ambush. I pan back to Irene Steele. She says, "Nobody got around to officially thanking Laura till 1860, when she was a very old and poor lady. One of the few things she left behind was this." She holds up a battered black...something. It clanks. "We don't have her cow," she says, and people laugh, "but this is her cow's bell." Everybody *oohs*. She waves it around. The bell clanks some more. "Maybe it's fitting that this simple sound is our connection to one of our earliest heroes. A hard and humble life was almost the only reward she had for bravery and loyalty in the face of great danger. It's the only reward of some women to this day. And now I'm happy to answer questions, and you make take pictures."

"Cut," I say.

"Good stuff," I hear Mark say. I lift the camera off my shoulder as Basil comes up.

"Get it?" he asks. He grins as I look back at him.

"I messed up the first pan," I tell him. "The rest should be okay."

"Let's have a look." Basil flips down a little viewer at the side of the camera and zips back through the footage. He starts the playback, and I lean in to look. It's me sitting on the platform. My legs are not sticks—they're toothpicks. I sigh as the camera pans to the next thrower. He's wearing a baby-blue *BREAD* T-shirt. "Hey!" I say as the hatchet spins toward the rope and slices it.

"I'll be right ba—" A hand clamps down on my shoulder.

"I thought that was you behind the camera," Grandpa says.

EIGHT

"Hi, Grandpa." I turn to him, and Grandpa starts to grin.

"Looks as if you're busy, Spence. Where's Bernard?"

"Oh. He was, uh, over there, at the hatchet-throw thing." I wave my hand. "He got me wet. I was just going to go get him."

"Tell you what," Grandpa says. "Why don't you go back to camp and put on some dry clothes? I'll show you how to get there. Those shorts look as if you've had an accident, if you get my drift. I'm sure Bernard knows to come here, right?"

"Yeah, for sure," I lie. Little lies I can manage, and hey, up till now I've told the truth, even when it hurt. I figure I'm allowed this one. "Um, this is Basil and Mark," I say. "I'm helping them film."

Mark stands up to shake hands with Grandpa. He starts grinning at me too. I seem to be a happy factory. As I wonder about this, Irene comes up. She slips an arm around Grandpa's waist and gives him a squeeze. "How was that?" she says.

Grandpa squeezes her back. "Irene, darling," he says, "you can still spin it with the best of them." Then they grin goofily at each other. Whoa! Let's just say I'm surprised. This would be embarrassing even if they weren't grandparents. It's time for me to get out of here before things get any ickier.

"Grandpa? How do I get back to camp?"

Grandpa lets go of Irene. He walks me past the cabin and points out the way. "It's not far," he says. "Put on some dry clothes and come right back. We're having supper over here with Irene, and she says there'll be entertainment after that.

I've brought your hoodies already, so I don't think you'll need anything else." He smiles at me. "Including your cell phone." I'd been wondering if I should ask for it. "Can you handle it?" Grandpa asks.

"Sure." I nod.

"Good man. I knew you could. One last thing. Stop off at the washroom and clean your face. And watch out for the P.I. See you soon."

I head off the way Grandpa told me, wondering why I have to clean my face. When I get around some more trees and some poison ivy, I see the road and the campsite, the Jeep and then our two tents. I duck inside the one Bunny and I are using. Our sleeping bags have been unrolled on the foam pads. Bun's is green, with cowboy pictures on the lining inside. Hey, he picked it. Mine is blue, with *Star Wars* designs. I think *Star Wars* is much cooler, but I don't say that around our older cousins, like Steve or DJ. They've got real camping gear.

There's a scrap of paper at the top of my sleeping bag. It's got printing on it, in crayon:

1 arm man has yor fone. Only Bun spells like that, especially in crayon. Sounds as if he thinks he's found my phone. Didn't I see a one-armed guy back at the splash platform? I'm definitely going to have to find Bunny before they both get a surprise from each other. Life is getting complicated when all I want to do is make Grandpa proud.

I grab my backpack and dig in, looking for my jeans. Mom must have packed my jeans. Except she didn't. Instead, she packed me a second pair of monster cargo shorts. I say a few more words I'm not supposed to know, then get changed and take the wet ones outside. I spread them on the hood of the Jeep to dry. Then I go to one of the side mirrors and look at my face. One eye has a big black circle around it. I look like half a raccoon with glasses. What the…? Then I remember Basil fooling with the camera and me shoving my eye right up to the viewfinder. Thanks, guys. I say more words I shouldn't know (actually, I repeat some because I don't know that many) and head for the washroom.

The public washroom is like the one near the Niagara College tent: a square brick building with windows set up high in the walls. This one has an extra sign pointing to showers. I pass that and go into the men's side to wash my face. It takes some scrubbing. When I finally get done, there are no paper towels. I'm not sticking my face in front of one of those dryer thingies, so I go into a stall for some toilet paper. As I do, I hear men's voices through the open window above me.

"…drives me crazy. It's so farb it's disgusting."

"Aw, it's not that bad. It's just a joke on the norms."

"It makes *all* of us look bad. It's a disgrace. Someone should do something about it. Now. This weekend."

"Like what? You can't just take—"

"Never mind what. All I'm saying is, it has to be stopped."

This sounds serious. Who's talking? The window is too high for me to see out of. Unless… I reach up, grab the windowsill and quietly step onto the toilet seat. I'm still not high enough, so I plant a foot on the chrome thingy that rises at the back, where the flush handle is attached. Balanced on one foot, I raise my head to peek through the window screen. Two men are standing in the shade, both wearing American-soldier uniforms. One of them is Luther Sideburns.

"Luther," the other guy says, "why don't you just talk to—"

"I've tried. It's useless," Luther snaps back.

"Maybe it's how you—"

"Excuse me!" another voice calls. "Could we get a picture?" A tourist couple walks up. He's got a fancy camera hanging around his neck.

"Sure can!" Suddenly Luther is all cheery. "Let's get in the sun, where the light's better."

The lady poses with Luther and the other reenactor. In the sunlight, her blond hair is so bright it almost hurts to look at it. Luther is blabbing away about their uniforms. The guy, who's Asian, fusses with his camera. "Tomato," he mutters. "Tomato, tomato, tomato." I have no idea what this means, but I wish he'd hurry up. It's really uncomfortable perching one-footed on top of a toilet-flusher post and clinging to a windowsill. I want them to get their picture fast and go away, so I can maybe learn more about what Luther is up to.

The photographer guy is still having camera problems. "Tomato!" he says louder. I wonder if this is his way of avoiding those words I'm not supposed to know. I know a kid at school who says *Stink!* all the time. I remember my own problems filming. Maybe I should switch words too.

After a couple more *tomatoes*, the guy snaps the picture. This is good, because my fingers are locking into claws on the windowsill and my foot is really hurting. I can't hang on here much longer. Finally, the couple wanders off. The second reenactor turns to Luther Sideburns.

"Luther," he says, "all I'm saying is, don't overreact. At the end of the day, it's just a hobby. Fun, remember?"

"It's not just a hobby. It's history. Whatever I do will be in the name of truth."

He marches off. My foot slips and hits the flush lever. It goes down and so do I, one foot in the toilet bowl as fresh water gushes in. "Tomato," I say. It doesn't help at all.

NINE

Grandpa doesn't ask me why I have a soaker, which is nice of him. Or maybe he doesn't notice. He and Irene Steele are sitting in camp chairs, sipping from paper cups and yakking up a storm. Irene has changed into jeans and a white sweater and white runners. "Surely that was in Budapest," she says with a laugh, acting like it's the funniest thing in the world again.

"My dear, I swear it was Vienna," Grandpa says loudly.

She tries again. "Casablanca?"

Grandpa smiles. "Like Rick—"

"And Ilsa," she finishes for him. "Poochy, that's so sweet."

Oh, *please.* Luckily, Tracey steps out of the cabin. She's changed back into normal clothes too. "Hey," she says. "Basil and Mark say you did great. They want to talk to you about helping some more."

I start to say okay, then remember what helping has gotten me so far. Besides, I may have other things to do now, things that would make Grandpa proud. That means I have to find Bun, in case I need help.

Tracey says, "Don't worry. We all got the camera trick played on us. It's an initiation to movies. Now you're in. Besides, this is a little more special. You might be the only one who can do it."

"Really?" I say. It's nice to hear you might be special.

"Let's go talk to them and find out."

"Well, I have to get my brother first—"

Grandpa interrupts. "Bernard won't be back for dinner, Spence. He was just here. He's busy with some friends he's made, and he'll join us later. Doing his thing, as they say. Independence is good."

Irene Steele smiles. "It was so nice to meet him. My, he has a deadpan sense of humour. He's such a card I almost believed he thought there was a real war on."

For a second I wonder if Bunny *does* think there's a real war on. I don't go there. All I say is, "Which way did he go?"

Grandpa waves across the encampment. "They went that way. You'll probably spot them."

"We're going to the equipment tent," Tracey says. "Food at seven, right? We'll see you there."

"TTFN," calls Irene Steele. She's topping up the paper cups with something from a thermos.

"Let's go," I say to Tracey. If Grandpa thinks independence is a good thing, just wait till I stop Luther.

My shoe really squelches as we walk. "How'd you get a soaker?" Tracey asks.

Should I tell her? I may need Tracey's help too—she knows way more about what's farb than I do. Besides, I was going to ask Bun for help. It will still count as independence as long as it's not Grandpa who's helping.

I tell her about the toilet and Luther Sideburns.

"Aw, really?" she says. "In the toilet? Bummer." At least she doesn't laugh. Even better, she goes on. "So Luther's mad again. I wonder what he's on about this time."

"It sounds as if he's going to do something bad. We have to stop him," I say.

Tracey frowns. "You know, Spencer, Luther's kind of an odd guy. You can see he takes things pretty seriously, but really he's mostly talk. Let's leave him alone and stick to the movie, huh?"

Before I can answer, the fiddle player joins us. His tall hat is pushed back, and wisps of damp hair stick to his forehead. "Off duty, Tracey?" he rumbles in a voice like a gravel road. "How's the movie coming?"

"Pretty good, Ken. Got a meeting right now. This is Spencer—he's helping."

"Spencer. Pleased to meet ya." We shake hands. It's like shaking a sweaty, midsized baseball glove. His blue coat looks pretty warm. Ken tells Tracey he's playing tonight at the campfire.

They chatter till we get to the Niagara College tent, so I never do answer Tracey. That's okay, because I don't think she would have liked my answer.

TEN

In the tent, all the Niagara film students are gathered around a monitor, watching what they've filmed. "We call these the rushes," Tracey explains. "We'll edit it down to the best bits later, then add music."

I watch the charge I thought I'd died in, the blacksmith making a horseshoe, the lady auctioning off her husband, the one-armed officer with the big mustache drilling Luther Sideburns and other bluecoat troops, another lady making candles, kids running along a path, rolling hoops by whacking them with sticks, redcoat Tracey showing how to load a musket, the fiddler mugging and playing. He's in a lot of the shots, in fact.

In some of them you see me too, because I'm the guy at the beginning with the clapperboard. I think I look pretty professional doing it, except for my stick legs and monster shorts. I'm pretty sure I spot Bunny a couple of times also, and then there he is for sure, in his *BREAD* shirt, throwing the hatchet. Beside him is a Native-looking kid who's definitely a reenactor. He's got no shirt, a Mohawk haircut and stripes of paint or something under his eyes. This must be one of his new friends. The kid's fist shoots up in the air as Bun's throw cuts the rope. Bun smiles his big happy smile. Then the camera pans, and I don't look so happy. I look like a drowned mound of baggy clothes with glasses. Everybody in the tent laughs, except me. "Great shot," someone says.

"Keeper!"

"Cut the pan, jump-cut to his face."

"Yeah, yeah, jump-cut. Love the reaction shot."

I don't. Luckily, we move on to where I filmed Irene Steele. That turned out great, except for the part where I blurt my magic words into the microphone. That gets another big laugh. Someone calls, "Ed-iiiiiiiiiit."

Tracey nudges me. "Don't worry. Easy fix. The really good stuff is when people forget to take their mics off and you hear them talking in a port-a-potty or someplace on the set."

Basil shuts down the playback. "So, we've got the battle tomorrow, and the transition shots."

They all talk boring stuff I don't understand about their project. I look out the open tent flap. The Native kid with the Mohawk haircut runs by. "Hey!" I jump up. Maybe Bunny is with him. As I start after him, I hear my name.

"So would that be okay, Spencer?"

"Huh?"

"You could help with that tomorrow? It wouldn't take long, but it would be huge for us. And only if we have to."

"Yeah, yeah, sure," I say. Tracey is looking at me funny, but I don't have time for this right now. I dash out of the tent.

The kid is gone. There's no Bunny either. In fact, there's not much of anyone. The fiddle music has finally stopped. The tourists have thinned down to a last few. Some redcoats and bluecoats are strolling along together. A few others I've seen in costumes have changed into normal clothes and are walking with lawn chairs and coolers. Everyone is drifting to the far end of the encampment. I follow them to a big space with picnic tables. There's a line of modern tents like ours and a parking lot farther down. At one side some musicians are setting up on a low stage. Smoke wafts from fire pits at the other side. Over one, a giant lump is being turned on a spit. Over another, something is being stirred in a monster pot hanging from a chain. Other people are laying out food on the picnic tables. All at once I'm starving. It feels as if we had that ice cream a million years ago. I also spot Luther, sideburns flaming, standing to one side and frowning at it all. He's still in uniform. Bun will be here somewhere, as hungry as I am. Behind me I hear a funniest-thing-in-the-world laugh, and here come Grandpa and Irene Steele. This is the place to be, and for once I'm in it.

ELEVEN

Grandpa and Irene Steele are carting a blanket and camp chairs with them, and Grandpa has his tote bag. A few steps behind them is Tracey, with a food cooler. Excellent.

"Lend a hand, Spence." I take a couple of the folded-up chairs from Grandpa. We go to a spot near the stage, spread out the blanket and set up the chairs.

"We're dining *alfresco*," announces Irene Steele.

Whatever. "What's in the cooler?" I ask Tracey.

"Good stuff."

I don't think so. Tracey takes out fancy crackers, caviar, which is black fish eggs, stinky blue cheese, those disgusting little weenies Deb calls *cocktail sausages*, olives, pickles and crusty rolls. How gross can you get? There aren't even any chips. And Grandpa, it turns out, has only brought a bottle of wine in his tote bag.

"Don't worry," Tracey says with a grin, passing me a fork and a paper plate. "Grab some real chow at the fire pits. That's what I'm doing."

"Are there hot dogs?"

"They're not exactly an 1812 thing, but yeah." She points at a group of picnic tables. "And that's potluck stuff to share."

I go over to join a line and find myself behind Ken the fiddler. "Hard to choose between the hog roast and the squirrel stew, isn't it?" He chuckles. "I'm having both."

I drop out of line and find a barbecue where the guy who coaxed me onto the water platform is cooking hot dogs. He gives me two, saying,

"Here's an extra for being a good sport. Got dried off?"

I think about my foot, but say yeah anyway.

"Good. Mustard and stuff thataway."

I load up my hot dogs with relish and ketchup for veggies, then round out my plate with chips and Cheezies. With a tin of ginger ale, it's a balanced meal. This is the best part of camping so far. I look around for Bunny, but he's still invisible. I'm too hungry to care. I go back to Grandpa and Irene. They're sipping wine and nibbling the alfresco stuff. "What about souvenir belt buckles?" Grandpa is asking.

"No one wears a belt, my darling. Everyone's pants are falling down these days."

"Then how about these?" Grandpa pulls something from his pocket. At first it looks like a chunk of rock. Then I see rounded points sticking out at odd angles, like a rusted star. "It's a caltrop. They also called it a crow's foot. Soldiers would scatter these on the ground to lame troops or horses that were moving toward them, injure their feet. No matter how it lands, see how there are always points sticking out or up? This one's all corroded, but the points were sharp and nasty when it was new. Got a guy in Taiwan who could run these up to look old or new. Manufacturing specs included. Have to decide on distribution. We call 'em Star Wars 1812. Could have them ready for the 2012 anniversary of the war. What do you think?"

Irene Steele holds the caltrop in her fingertips and cocks an eyebrow. Grandpa says slowly, "This is the real deal, just for you. They're quite rare. Call it a reminder of shared adventures."

She weighs the caltrop in her fingertips and gives Grandpa a look. "Poochy, how sweet. I knew I could count on you. It's a *pointed* reminder."

"Maybe you'll find investors."

She arches that eyebrow again. "Who could there be but you?" They lean forward and tap their paper cups together in a toast. Then they lean even closer. I take off with my food before there's smooching. Ancient-people romance is even worse than fish eggs.

Where can I go? Bunny is still Mr. Invisible. I spot Tracey and her movie friends. They're in a huddle, and there's a new girl with them. She's small and really pretty, with long brown hair, and she's waggling car keys in one hand. She doesn't look happy. As I get close I hear her say, "Well, I don't care if it's just a costume. How did you *think* I'd feel about it? It's still total exploitation of animals. I'm an ethical vegan, Basil. You already know that!"

I guess she's found out the dinner choices are roast hog or squirrel stew. Basil is saying to her, "I know, I know, Stef—just asking. We've planned around that anyway." He looks up and spots me. "Still good for tomorrow, Spencer?"

I nod.

"Good. Seven thirty, at the tent."

No one is inviting me to stay. I keep moving. A second later I barely keep my plate from flipping over. Sitting on a log a few meters away is Luther Sideburns.

I know Tracey says he's all talk and to leave him alone, but I still have this feeling he's really up to something. Grandpa said independence is a good thing, right? Maybe I can find out on my own.

I make my feet take me over to the log. I probably look as if I'm walking on caltrops. I sit down. Luther looks at me and nods. Up close, he's thin faced and pointy nosed, and his sideburns are truly gigantic, like huge orange squirrel tails on his cheeks. His tall hat sits at his feet. His shapeless clodhopper boots and white pants are dirty.

How do adults talk? I take a bite of hot dog and go for it. "Good day?" I hope Luther doesn't notice my little spray of relish. He nods and keeps eating, his sideburns wiggling as he chews. He's got a tin cup to drink from, a hunk of cheese, some kind of biscuit that looks like cement and, stuck on a knife, a dead something I think is beef jerky. I try again. "Aren't you having any squirrel stew?"

Luther shakes his squirrel tails. "It's not really squirrel. It's beef." He sounds disgusted.

"I guess that's pretty farb, huh?"

He nods, then waves the dead thing on a knife at me. "Go hardcore or go home." The knife looks definitely hardcore.

"Oh. Sorry," I say and look at my hot dogs.

"Nah, it's fine for you," Luther says. "You're not one of us. I like a tube steak myself when I'm not doing this."

"Reenacting?"

"*Not* that word—I hate it. I'm an *interpreter*. I bring history back to life."

"Like Frankenstein?" I know that's a dumb one as soon as I say it.

Luther frowns. "No. That's what farbs do. They make something like history, but distorted. I do the real thing. Look at these buttons."

He tugs at his uniform coat. "These boots. *Exact* replicas. Custom made."

Actually, I think the boots look like Frankenstein's, but I don't say that. "Back then," Luther goes on, "they didn't make right- and left-foot patterns, just straight boots. They hurt like hell until you get used to them. But you get farbs showing up in their Blundstones, for crying out loud. You've got girls in the ranks pretending to be soldiers. You've got guys"—he grips a squirrel-tail sideburn—"who *glue on* side whiskers like Elvis impersonators or something. Some of us don't take our duty to history seriously enough." Luther is getting seriously worked up. "And some of us"—he leans forward, pointing at me with the knife and dead thing—"even mislead people. On purpose." He tears a hunk of dead thing off with his teeth and starts chewing. The sideburns go crazy.

I myself stop chewing. This could be my chance. I lean forward too, trying to ignore the knife. "Who? How?"

Luther's eyes narrow. Everything about him seems to be pointing now. He growls, "There's this—" He stops. "Skip it. No offense, but you're not one of us. There are ways of dealing with it in-house."

"How?" I whisper.

"Let's just say Yankee ingenuity." Luther sits back, nodding to himself. He takes a last swig from his cup, then begins stuffing things into his pack. "Hey, weekdays I'm a dentist in Rochester, a precision kind of guy. I owe that to my patients. I owe it to history too."

I try again. "So, like, what would be misleading?"

"Like I said, anything fake. And making up stories. I mean, you Canadians won't even admit we won the War of 1812."

"You did?"

"Of course we did. Everybody knows that." Luther wipes the knife blade on his pants.

"So something Canadian is farb?"

"What's bugging me is."

"My grandpa has a genuine caltrop."

Luther looks up fast. "Really? Those are scarce as hen's teeth."

"Is that a dentist joke?"

His eyebrows scrunch. "No, it's an old saying. I'd love to see it."

I'm thinking fast now. "Well, he'd probably let you. But he's Canadian, and we'd want to know what farb Canadian thing is bugging you. Maybe we could do something about it."

"Well…" says Luther.

"Or you could just tell me."

Luther frowns and scratches the bare chin between his squirrel tails.

"You never know," I coax.

Luther thinks it over some more. "Where's your granddad?"

I point. "He's over there." Luther turns, and I add, "With Irene Steele."

Luther scrambles up and hoists his pack. "Forget it."

"What?" I say. "Why?"

"Just forget it. I'll handle it myself." Then he clamps his mouth shut hard enough to crack his own teeth.

Somehow I've blown it. As Luther shoulders his pack, I blather, "Hey, you could have been a dentist back then. Why don't you, I mean, maybe you could act—I mean, interpret—"

Luther shakes his head, but he stops scowling. He switches into something like Grandpa's lecture mode. "There weren't any dentists. Dental hygiene was *terrible* in those days. No money in it either. Get your teeth pulled by some drunk with a pair of pliers. And pig-bristle toothbrushes! You could get anthrax from the brush, for crying out loud. Or dentures from dead people's teeth—think about that. Nah, I'm a big fan of paychecks and antibiotics. And some of your advanced tartar removers now do a great job of shining buckles and buttons too. Saves on polishing." He puts on his tall hat. "Weekend warrior only," he says from under his chin strap. "When I get home

I'll have hot dogs. Right now I want the real deal. I'm off to picket duty. Enjoy." He nods and clomps off. I wonder if I remembered to pack my toothbrush.

TWELVE

I'm kind of glad Luther is gone. Tracey was right about him. Jer would call him *intense*, which Jer is not. Also, I can't stop thinking about dentures made from dead people's teeth. Suddenly I'm not hungry anymore.

But is he really going to do something? And to whom? For sure he doesn't like Irene Steele, even though she's got Laura Secord's real cowbell, and that's got to be the least farby thing here— even rarer that a caltrop. Is it because she talks about a battle the Americans lost? That's not farb though.

Then it hits me that maybe it's not just Irene Steele. Maybe it's Tracey too: Luther doesn't like girl soldiers. Tracey says Luther is all talk, but it sounds like more than that to me. Man, I wish Bun was here to talk this over with. He's smarter than people think. Sometimes it helps to see things differently.

I dump what's left of dinner in a trash bin and go looking for Bunny again. The sun is just starting to tuck behind the trees. A mosquito hums by my ear, and then music starts up from the stage, drumming and fiddles and lots of whooping. People start clapping along. Grandpa and Irene aren't. I think they're maybe holding hands between the chairs. I don't go for a closer look.

Tracey and her friends are setting up to do some filming. "We can't light it," someone says. "The generator will be louder than the band."

"Bring the white van up from the parking lot and shine the high beams from Mark's car on the side. That should reflect enough light."

"Yeah, if we parked the car in the middle of the crowd. They'd love that."

"Stage light and firelight. Underexposed is good—moody atmosphere."

I leave them to argue.

The evening is getting cool as I walk. I know Grandpa brought hoodies for us, but I don't really want to go back there right now. It's not just the hand-holding. I don't want to be the kid who sits with the grown-ups because there's nothing else to do. I'm supposed to be independent.

I wander down to the parking lot, then back up to where a line of modern tents is pitched. No Bunny. Past those is a neat square of old-fashioned ones—wedge tents, Tracey called them, part of the reenactment. Luther is standing over there, one foot forward, musket cradled in his arms. His pants and crossed white belts seem to glow in the twilight. I guess picket duty is like standing guard. I think he should give it up for the night. Nobody's paying attention, and the only thing to guard against is probably skunks.

He looks more like a kid sulking at a party than a soldier.

Ken the fiddler is having a beer with some people. His fiddle lies on the picnic bench in front of him. Like Luther, he's still wearing his costume. "Spencer," he calls. "You look a little lost, man."

I tell him I'm looking for Bunny. Ken hasn't seen him. "But I love the *BREAD* T-shirt," he rumbles. "I confess I might have had one myself." He asks how I got to help Tracey, and I explain about Grandpa knowing Irene Steele. "They're nice folks," says Ken. "That's a great routine she's got about the cowbell, huh?" He chuckles. "You know, sometimes I wonder if she's as deaf as she lets on. She can be a pretty fast twitch when she needs to be. More schtick, I guess. Speaking of which"—he drains his beer and heaves himself up from the table—"time for me to go onstage for my special guest appearance." Before I can ask him more about Irene, he's headed for the stage.

I follow him through the crowd. It's almost completely dark now. There are lots of people here, their faces lit by campfires and the stage lights. In a pause between songs I hear someone say, "Speed!" Part of the movie crew must be filming. I wish things would speed up for me somehow. I mean, I'm glad this isn't your regular fishing-and-poison-ivy camping trip, but I'm not sure what it's become instead, except that I seem to be alone in it.

Back at Grandpa and Irene's spot, the chairs are empty. Our hoodies are folded on one of them, with a flashlight and a note on top. It's definitely a day for notes.

Spence & Bernard
All well. Helping Irene. Back very soon.
Sit tight or remember we meet at camp by 10:00.
Have fun.
Grandpa

Ten? What time is it now? If I had my phone I'd know, wouldn't I? And where is everybody? I tug on my hoodie, then don't know what to do except wish Bun was around. It's not as if we're Siamese twins or anything, but I'm getting bugged that he's just taken off without me, even if he thinks he's after my phone. Although I guess that's what I did to him this aft, and I wasn't bugged when I was busy filming. Now, though, I could tell him I found the phone. He could show me how to throw a hatchet. Maybe we could figure out Luther Sideburns.

But I already said I should do this alone, show Grandpa I'm independent, right? Maybe I'm grumpy because I'm still hungry.

I *am* hungry. I wish I hadn't ditched the rest of my dinner. I know we've got food in the Jeep, but it's dark now, and a long way back to our campsite, and besides, the Jeep is locked. I checked when I looked at myself in the side mirror. I look in Irene's food cooler instead. There's an empty cracker box and a plastic container with two wrinkled olives and some cocktail weenies. Yuck.

Up on the stage, Ken the fiddler is playing a tiny old guitar and making faces like all Three

Stooges at once. I decide to take one last look for Bun—and for any chow that might still be on the potluck tables.

I rustle up some damp potato chips, but no Bunny. I'm near the parking lot when something stops me. Over by the ghostly white blobs of the reenactor tents where Luther Sideburns was standing guard, a smaller white blob is gliding away. I think Luther's on the move.

THIRTEEN

I'm running after him before I even know it.
I don't know what I'm going to do, and I don't
know what he's going to do, but I have a feeling
this is it. I cut the distance between us, then slow
down—I don't want him to hear footsteps.

Away from the fires and stage lights, stars
and a chunk of moon shine enough for me
to make out the white pants and belts of his
uniform. The darker shape of his head seems
ten feet tall, so he must be wearing his hat too.
I pull my hood up and slow down even more.

I bet my bare legs show in the dark. I promise myself I will never ever wear cargo shorts again, no matter what.

I'm following just close enough to hear the swish of Luther's heavy boots through the grass as he strides past the reenactor tents. A waxy smell hangs in the air. In one tent, a light glows through the canvas. My guy stays well away from it. I creep past.

We leave the white tents behind, and I follow him along a line of trees. My foot crunches a stick. I gasp and sink into the shadows. Luther's head half turns, but he's in shadow too, and under the hat brim all I see is a pale blur of face. He keeps moving.

I let him get farther ahead as we cross an open space. It looks as if we're headed for the modern tents the non-hardcores have set up. I'm pretty sure he doesn't have his musket. That makes me feel better until I remember his knife. I take a second to remind myself that Luther Sideburns is a dentist from Rochester, not a rogue 1812 soldier. Then I remember my last dentist visit. That doesn't help.

Now he's reached the line of tents. He slows down too. These tents are like ours, and most of them are dark. I'm guessing their owners are still over at the stage. I'm also guessing Luther Sideburns is going to sneak into one of those dark ones and—and what? Steal something? Wreck something? And here's another question. How do I stop him?

I duck behind a tree near the first tent. He keeps on slowly, almost as if he's counting the tents. It's hard to follow him from where I'm hiding. I can barely see the darker shadow of his tall hat above the tent flies. Voices murmur nearby; someone chuckles. Then the darkness of Luther's hat swoops down and I hear the quick *zzzzzzip* of a tent flap being opened.

As fast as I can, I tiptoe out from behind the tree and along the line of tents after him. But now my angle has changed, and the tents all seem the same shape and size. Light glows dimly in a red one and in a blue one next to it, both right about where Luther ducked down. The flaps are closed. Which one is he in? What should I do? All I can think is that I have to stall him before he does something bad—and maybe get a little help at the same time. Since I don't have a SWAT team or a police helicopter with a spotlight or a phone to call for help with or a nearby brother, I do the only thing I can think of.

I creep behind the tents. They're the kind held up by those snap-together bendy poles that curve into an X at the top. Rustling noises come from both tents. Which one is Luther in? Time could be running out. If I'm going to stop him and at least have a witness, I have to do it now. So I do. I take a deep breath and dash past the backs of the tents, yanking out the pegs and poles as I do.

They collapse like old gum bubbles. Voices shout, using some of the words I'm not supposed to know, and the fallen fabric pops and ripples like boiling oil. Then it erupts, and I'm caught square in the crossed beams of two flashlights, one from each tent. I don't even try to run. I've already frozen at the sound of the voices. One is Irene Steele's. One is Grandpa's. I don't know who owns the third one, but it's not Luther Sideburns. I've been following the wrong man.

FOURTEEN

"Care to explain this, Spence?" Grandpa's voice, coming from behind one of the flashlights, has gone dangerously flat again.

"You know this kid? What the hell is going on?" comes the reenactor's voice from behind the other flashlight. Now a third light pops on, thanks to Irene Steele, I guess, and I see that the guy isn't even an *American* soldier—his coat is red. Irene bellows, "I'm so sorry. A harmless prank. He was looking for us, I'm sure."

"My grandson," Grandpa says.

"I thought you were Luther," I blurt for no good reason.

"That American hardcore?" the reenactor snorts. "You nuts? He sleeps in a bedroll in the trees somewhere. He wouldn't use a tent like this."

"I thought I was going to catch him being farb." It's the best I can do.

Irene cuts in. "I don't know about ketchup on a farm, Spencer dear. We'll sort that later. Right now let's help set this lovely man's tent to rights."

There's a pause while we make sense of that, and then we do what Irene suggests and set the tents back up. The reenactor is pretty nice about the whole thing. "Good luck finding that Luther guy farbing," he says to me. "If you do, be sure to get a picture of it. He'd never live it down."

Grandpa doesn't say much while we fix things up. This is not a good sign. Also, his white hair sticks out at odd angles from under his beret, and his shirttail is hanging out. Grandpa is usually a tidy guy, so these are not good signs either.

I figure this is not the time to say what I was really doing. I'll tell Tracey tomorrow maybe—if I'm not grounded.

We walk back to the stage to collect Irene's chairs and stuff. No one says much. The show seems to be ending. We join a stream of people heading for the tents. I straggle along. Everything I've done today has been doomed from the start: first the cell phone, then trying to find it, then getting tricked into that raccoon eye from the camera and now this whole stupid Luther thing. Every time I've tried something on my own, I've blown it.

And here's the weird thing. If you'd asked me before we left if I wanted to be grounded in my tent all weekend, I'd have said, "Totally! Just leave me my phone and some comics." Not anymore. Now I want to help with the movie tomorrow. I want to get Bun to help me mess up Luther. And what makes it worst of all is that I've been trying so hard to do the kind of stuff Grandpa wants. It's not fair.

Back at her tent, Irene gives Grandpa a hug goodnight, then laughs and tries to smooth some of his wild hair. She looks a little messy herself. I guess I would too if a tent fell on me. "Good night, Spencer." She shakes my hand. "You know, being around you is a bit like being around your grandfather in the old days. Things tend to happen. But that's good. I've always liked fireworks, haven't I, Poochy?"

Grandpa grins and nods. "Without a doubt."

"Till tomorrow then." She slips inside her tent.

Yeah right, I think. I'm as much like Grandpa as sticking your foot in a toilet is like setting off fireworks. At least I don't feel my soaker anymore. Now both feet are wet with dew.

Grandpa and I start for our own campsite. Other people are headed that way too. Flashlights bob and weave in the dark. We haven't gone far when I feel Grandpa's hand, heavy on my shoulder. "Spence," he says sadly, and I figure this is it. "Spence, I owe you an apology. I completely understand why you did that with the tents. I'd have done the same thing myself."

"*You would?*"

"Damn straight. Independence is good, but I pushed it too hard. You and Bernard must have thought I just wanted you out of my hair—what there is of it—all day. That's not the case. And I shouldn't have iced the cake by going off like that with Irene."

I'm stunned. I manage to say, "That's okay, Grandpa."

"No, it's not okay. You were right to bring the house down. I apologize. It won't happen again." He squeezes my shoulder. "I don't know how you tracked us down, but we're all entitled to a few secrets, aren't we? Anyway, let's finish up the day together. You hungry?"

"Oh, yeah."

"Me too. Starved. Let's head to the Jeep and grab a snack."

FIFTEEN

Back at our campsite, Grandpa unlocks the Jeep and we climb in. He leaves the overhead light on. We open the windows partway to let cooler air in. "Bernard should be along any minute," Grandpa says. "He might want a bite too."

We open the food cooler and rustle up peanut-butter sandwiches, OJ, chips and cold hot dogs with no buns. "This is more like it," Grandpa says. "I hate those cocktail weenies, and I've never much liked caviar. Used to have to eat it doing business with the Russians and such. Irene could always pack it away." He chuckles.

"Her vodka too, if she needed to seal a deal. She was a pro."

We sit there munching away in the watery yellow light of the Jeep and waving away the occasional mosquito. Apart from when I was filming, this is the best I've felt all day. I like being with Grandpa when we just sit and talk. Not lecture mode, just talking, the two of us or with Bun. That doesn't happen very often. Our cousins like action stuff with him—boating and tubing, flying in his plane, skiing and sports. And when there are lots of people around, he can be kind of bossy. He has this trick he does at the cottage where he makes water spill into your lap at supper if you're not paying attention. But sometimes when we were littler he'd sit on the dock with us and tell stories from being in the war and working all around the world. Or at home we'd sit on the couch together and watch Bugs Bunny cartoons. His favorite was the one about the guy who finds the frog that sings and dances, but only for him. Grandpa can do an excellent Donald Duck voice too. We haven't done those things for a long time.

Grandpa passes me another hot dog and tops up my juice. "So you liked the movies, Spence?"

I nod as I chew. "I liked running the camera. Apart from the black eye."

Grandpa smiles and sips his juice. "Paying your dues. Don't want to be an actor?"

"Nope. I think if you're running the camera, you're the boss. I don't want to be the guy who gets soaked."

"Point taken. And it looked as if you knew what you were doing there."

That feels good to hear. I nibble some hot dog. They're good cold—chewier somehow. Grandpa says, "When I was a few years older than you, I had a crush on a girl who went on to be in the movies. At least, I'm pretty sure she did."

"Wow," I say. "You know a movie star?"

"No, no." Grandpa shakes his head. "Only knew her briefly. She left and I discovered airplanes and right off knew I wanted to fly.

Funny how you never can tell what's going to change your life, or where you'll find it." Grandpa digs another hot dog out of the pack. "I met a couple of other movie people through work over the years. I'm told it's a tough business."

"I said I'd help again tomorrow morning."

"Fair enough," says Grandpa, waving away a mosquito. "A real campfire breakfast in the morning. Then you do your filming, and we'll all do some things together. Watch that mock battle." Grandpa rubs his chin and smiles. "You know, I've been thinking about it and now I'm half wondering if Bernard thinks there's a real war on."

He looks at me. I remember Irene Steele said something about that too. Bun can for sure get funny ideas sometimes. Then again, I remember thinking I'd been shot. That embarrasses me though, so I shrug and say, "Why would he think that?"

If Grandpa says, *Maybe he thought the musket fire was real,* I'll laugh and say, *Oh, yeah, that happened to me, too. But he'd know it was fake pretty fast,* because I did. And he would too. Instead, Grandpa shrugs back. "I don't know either, Spence. But remind me to—"

There's a *thud* and a scratching noise outside. Instantly, Grandpa has the Jeep's light off and his flashlight on. Eyes gleam back at us through the windshield. A raccoon is perched on the hood. Grandpa laughs and switches the lights back on. "Make sure we put the windows up when we turn in. Speaking of which, what time do you help in the morning?"

"Seven thirty." All at once I'm tired.

"I'll wake you if you're not up." Grandpa checks his watch. "You get turned in. I'll wait for Bernard. I'm surprised at him. He knows better than to be this late." He opens the storage compartment between the seats and hands me a little flashlight. I'm about to remind Grandpa that Bunny doesn't have a watch when I see something else in there—my cell phone. Speaking of telling time...

"I'll make sure the coon is gone," Grandpa says. He flicks the overhead-light control off and opens his door. "You hit the hay. Give your teeth a dry brush."

His door closes. The instant the light blinks off, I grab my phone. "All clear," Grandpa says. I hop out too and duck into the tent. I can't help thinking how Grandpa's voice was getting stern again talking about Bun being late. Maybe it's time to cover for my brother, especially if he thinks he's rescuing my cell phone. I may not be good at lying, but maybe I can make this work. I grab some clothes from Bun's backpack and quickly stuff them and the pack and the pillow into a huddled lump in his sleeping bag, so it looks as if he's in there. Then I poke my head back out the tent flap and hiss, "Hey, Grandpa? Bun—*Bernard*'s already here. He's been asleep all the time."

Grandpa walks over with the flashlight, a tall darker shape in all the other shadows. I flick my light on for a second. "See?" Then I flick it off fast.

"He must have been bushed," Grandpa says. "Try not to wake him. Get into bed. You've got an early morning."

I zip the flap shut behind him. A second later I hear his tent being zipped open. In the dark I kick off my shoes and socks and scramble into my sleeping bag. I feel for my backpack and put my glasses on top of it. I check my shorts pocket for my phone. It's there. Through the tent wall I can see the glow of Grandpa's flashlight in his tent. Then I hear rustling noises and a big sigh and his flashlight goes out. "All good, Spence?" he calls softly.

"All good," I call softly back. "Good night, Grandpa."

"Good night, Spence."

Then I almost blow it. I forget Bun is supposed to be asleep and say into my pillow, muffling my voice, "Good night, Grandpa."

"Bernard?"

"Sorry, Grandpa, I guess I woke him."

"That's okay, Spence. Good night, Bernard."

"Good night, Grandpa." I do Bun again.

"Good night."

"Good night, Grandpa." Now I'm me.

"Good *night,* Spence."

"Good night." I shut up and settle in to wait for Bun. I have to tell him I've got my phone and get him to help me with Luther Sideburns. I hope he gets back soon, but not before Grandpa starts to snore. The last thing I remember before I fall asleep is that I left my wet shorts to dry on the hood of the Jeep, right about where the raccoon was. I hope it eats them.

SIXTEEN

I wake to sunshine glowing through the tent wall and the sound of Grandpa muttering more words I'm not supposed to know. Then a car door slams. My phone shows me it's 7:05. I wriggle out of my sleeping bag, and that's when I notice Bun's is wide-open. Everything I stuffed in it is scattered on the tent floor. Bun must have gotten back after I fell asleep and taken off again this morning. Why didn't he wake me? Now I can't tell him anything.

Grandpa turns as I crawl outside. He's standing beside the Jeep, holding a big cloth.

"Morning, Spence." He scratches his head. He's got the fishing hat on again. "Got a little hitch in our breakfast plans. Guess what I forgot to do last night?"

"Brush your teeth?" I suggest, remembering what I forgot to do.

Grandpa gives me a crooked smile. "I wish. Nope, I forgot to close the Jeep windows. Our raccoon buddy slipped in and helped himself."

I walk over and peek into the Jeep. "Wow." It's the only word I can think of. The cooler is tipped over on the backseat, and what's left of our food is everywhere else. The chip bag dangles from the turn indicator, a piece of bacon from the mirror. Eggshells litter the front seats. A chunk of hot dog balances on the stick shift, and something brown and yucky is spread on everything, including the windows, where it forms little paw prints. I don't want to ask, but I do anyway. "What's the, uh…"

"Peanut butter." Grandpa sighs. "The ants have already gotten in it." He waves the cloth at the car. "Tell Bernard it'll be a bare-bones breakfast.

We'll go somewhere for chow after I clean this mess up."

"He's already gone," I say. "And I have to go too. The movie."

Grandpa nods. "Right. There's still some milk in a thermos and some cereal. Let's get you set up." He tosses the cloth, already smeared with food, on the ground. I look closer. "Hey," I say. "My shorts!"

"What? Oh, sorry, Spence. They're all I've got to wipe up with. I'll get you new ones."

"Believe me, Grandpa, it's okay. Do you want these ones too? I could wear my swimsuit."

Too bad he says no. Grandpa rustles me up some cereal. We agree to meet at Irene Steele's reenactor cabin as soon as I'm done filming, and we'll all go for brunch. I take off for the Niagara College tent. My phone clunks comfortingly against my knee in a cargo pocket. I figure Grandpa will be too busy cleaning to look in the seat compartment. If he does, I can always say the raccoon must have taken it and

I found it on the ground. I know, I know, but I *did* get away with the fib about Bunny.

At the tent, most of the movie people are already there. From the way they look I'm guessing they're not what Jer would call *morning people*. There are a lot of takeout coffees. A couple of guys are moaning about how much beer they drank last night. Tracey walks over, carrying a camera. "I was hoping you'd come," she says. "You sure you want to do this?"

"Totally," I say. I hope the camera she's holding is for me to use. Or maybe Mark will show me how to do sound.

"Well, you sure are a good sport, Spencer."

"Spencer!" Basil hurries up. He's with Stef, the short pretty girl who showed up last night, the one with long brown hair. "Thanks so much for this, bud. We have to roll, like, ASAP before we lose the light. Come on in, and we'll do wardrobe."

"Wardrobe?"

"Yeah, we talked about this yesterday, remember? When we were watching the rushes.

You were good with it. We have the costume right here. You and Stef are about the same size, so it should work great." He's got my arm, dragging me into the tent.

"I really, really appreciate this," Stef says to me. "As an ethical vegan I just can't do it, you know? It's like…it's animal *exploitation*." Before I can ask *what* is animal exploitation, Basil is pulling clothes from a box in a corner of the tent. He holds them up to my shoulders. "Perfect!"

I look down. It takes me a second to realize I'm looking at a long pioneer dress, kind of like Irene Steele's. "What the—" I splutter. "What are—"

"Lift your arms so it's easier to put on," coaches Stef.

I'm too confused to stop myself. "But—" The dress comes down over my head, and for a second everything is a blind tangle. "My glasses," I yell.

"Hang on, hang on."

My head pops out, glasses still on. The dress drops to my middle, and then Basil is stuffing my hands in the sleeves and Stef is tugging down the bunched-up material at my waist. She pulls some kind of sash strings and ties them tight behind my back. "Fantastic," she says. "Look, you can't even see your shoes. You can keep them on."

I look down again. My stick legs and monster shorts have disappeared behind a waterfall of fabric printed with little pink flowers. "Ew," I say. "I didn't say anything about doing this. I thought—"

"Spencer." Basil cuts me off. "Spence, buddy. Listen, man. This is our only chance to get this footage, with the reenactors and everything. It's the key to the whole movie, and you're our only hope. Stef would do it, but she's got issues—"

"*Ethics*, Bas. I'm an ethical vegan."

"Whatever. Please, Spencer. Nobody will even see your face. No one will know it's you."

"But this is so dumb. I don't look like a girl," I complain.

"You will in a sec," Stef says. She straps padding across my *ELO* shirt and fastens it at my back.

"Aw, come on!" I squirm.

"Hold still," she orders. "Pull up the top." She and Basil pull the dress up to my neck. I see it has a frilly white collar and more frills at the cuffs. Stef tugs it tight, and I feel her hooking fasteners up my back. I squirm some more. It doesn't help. "There," she says, stepping back to look. "Perfect."

"It is not," I say. "It's stupid. And what about my face? And my glasses? I'm not wearing some dumb wig either."

"You don't have to," says Basil, and he jams a monster bonnet onto my head. He ties the strings under my chin. "Excellent. Your mom wouldn't even know it was you. We'll have the cow ready for you in a minute."

SEVENTEEN

The bonnet has a brim that curves around my face down to my chin. I can't see anything at my sides, and I can't hear so great either. It feels as if I'm looking out of a train tunnel. Stef has to steer me a little to get me out of the tent. "Cow?" I'm saying. "What cow?"

Tracey appears in front of me. The camera is on her shoulder. "Wow," she says. "You look good."

I remember what I was looking at when I said *wow* this morning. "I do not look good. I can't believe I'm doing this."

"Well, you make a convincing girl."

I so do not want to hear *that,* so I pretend I didn't. "What are they talking about, a cow?"

"You have to lead the cow," Tracey says. "But don't worry, it's not the real cow from yesterday. It's just two guys in a cow costume. The real one is afraid of gunfire."

"Gunfire?" *I'm* afraid of gunfire. "What do I have to do?"

"Didn't Basil explain? You're playing Laura Secord. Remember, from yesterday? We need to film Laura walking all around the reenactment, almost like a time traveler. She connects everything together. Stef can do that for us. But first we need the most important part—Laura leads her cow through the smoke of battle as if it's 1812, and they emerge in the present day. She's kind of a symbol. You know symbolism?"

I nod. "Like a drummer?"

Tracey looks confused. Then she says, "No, Spencer, not drum cymbals. Symbolism is… never mind. You just have to lead the cow around the reenactor battle. Get in the smoke. Then we'll put the costume on Stef, and she can do the rest, without the cow. And don't worry, I'm filming. I'll never show your face or your glasses."

"So I just walk around the battle? I sort of hoped I could do some filming today. Or sound."

"Soon as we're done these shots, Spencer, I promise you can. Let's just get this done first. Basil's right—we really need this. It's the most important part."

Mark swings into my tunnel vision, blocking out Tracey. He kneels in front of me and clips something to my dress, near the hem. Then he reaches under the dress and runs his hand up my leg. "Hey!" I jump back.

"Geez, Spencer, hold still." I feel him fumbling with the pocket near the bottom of my monster shorts. "I've gotta get the power pack for the mic in there." Something heavy bumps the side of my knee. "Bingo. Now don't trip on the cord, whatever you do." Mark fumbles at the hem of my dress. *My* dress? I mean, the dress that I'm wearing.

"I'll just pin it like this. See?" He holds up the fabric. I see the black wire running to the little clip-on mic.

"I have to say stuff too? To way down there? I'll have to yell, and I don't sound like a girl. Maybe I should just—"

"You don't say anything," Mark assures me. "All I want is your footsteps. Hang on." He pulls his headphones on over his ballcap and clicks at his little computer. "Okay, walk around for me."

I walk across the grass. Somewhere behind me a voice screeches, "Help!" I spin toward the tent. Was that Bunny's voice? Mark calls, "Perfect, Spencer," and then Basil has my elbow, hustling me away. At least, I think it's Basil. It's his voice talking to me.

"But," I say, "I think I heard—"

Basil keeps talking. "Okay, Spencer, here's the scene. You're wandering, in a dream, leading the cow. All around you the War of 1812 is raging, but you don't hear any of it. You drift through the smoke and the battle. Don't hurry—try to float along. You can't rush the cow anyway. It's really hard for the guys in the cow costume to see where they're going, so just lead them gently with the rope. Okay, let's see you float."

"Huh?"

"Walk for me."

I do what I'm told. I want to get this over with and get back to look for Bunny. "Hold your dress up a little with one hand," Basil calls. "No, lower—we can see your runners. C'mon, Spencer, glide. Float for us, baby! Okay, stop!"

Basil runs up to me. "Beautiful." He points to the open area ahead. Ranks of redcoats and bluecoats are forming on opposite sides. "Okay, the reenactors are setting up there, tourists are on that side only…" He turns me, and I see a crowd already waiting. A bunch of them have cameras set up on tripods. One of them is Tomato Guy. Basil goes on. "Stay away from them. When it starts, you go up this other side, where the fighting will be. Try to get into the smoke, and try not to react to the noises, okay? Remember, it's a dream. Go slow. Tracey will be shooting with the handheld the whole time, and Mark will be with her. Don't worry about where she is. When you get to the trees, stay on this side, in the sunlight. It's too dark to shoot in there. Got it?"

I nod. I still want to find Bun. "Yeah, but I've gotta—"

"Gotta what?" says Basil. Before I can answer, he says, "Oh, for sure. The port-a-potties are right over there. We've got a good ten minutes to wait."

Actually, now that I think of it, I do have to go, kind of. I hustle over and join a lineup of redcoats and bluecoats. They're all joking with each other about aiming high. When one of them says, "Ladies first" to me and lets me go ahead, I don't bother to argue. Maybe this way I'll have time to get back and find Bun.

Using a port-a-potty is tricky when you're wearing a pioneer dress and monster cargo shorts *and* a clip-on microphone. I remember what Mark said about mics and port-a-potties and keep my mouth shut. When I step out, Mark is waiting. "It's time."

EIGHTEEN

The cow is standing by Basil and Tracey. It looks—surprise, surprise—a lot like two guys in a cow costume. Maybe from a distance, with the smoke and everything, it won't matter. Maybe they can fix it with computers later. Maybe this will make vegans happier. Who knows? It's not my problem. I just want to do my dream glide, find Bunny and move on.

Tracey hands me the end of a rope tied around the cow's neck. "Just waiting for the start," she says.

"Don't you want to be reenacting?" I ask. "Battles must be the best part."

"Not really," she says. "They're loud and confusing, and everybody argues about who has to die. I'd rather do demonstrations and talk to tourists. But making a movie is more fun than either one."

Behind me, something clanks. Basil says, "Perfect." I turn. A black bell is hanging from the cow's neck. I say to Tracey, "Is that your Laura Secord bell?"

Tracey nods. "I didn't think Gram would mind as long as we get it back in time for her talk. Maybe it'll make the cow a little more authentic. Hey, speaking of which, did I see you talking with Hardcore Luther at supper last night?"

"Oh. Yeah. I need to tell you, I don't think he likes your family very much. He was all worked up about farb stuff and Canadians and especially your gram. I really think he's going to do something."

Tracey sighs. "Spencer, this is Luther's idea of *doing something*: one time last year he tried to mess up Gram by demonstrating how to load and fire his musket right across from her while she was talking. And he totally blew it because he got four pan flashes in a row."

"What?"

"A musket fires when a spark strikes a little pan of gunpowder and sets it off. That fires the cartridge. But a lot of times it doesn't go off. There's just a flash in the pan and nothing happens. It's a total drag when you're demon-strating. So Luther got four misfires in a row. The last try, he was so mad he forgot to do the tap test to make sure he'd taken the ramrod out of the barrel. The musket fired and shot the ramrod right into a tree. Talk about a farb thing to do. He was lucky he didn't get sent home for that."

"So he's really not worth worrying about?" I think about how I spent yesterday evening.

Tracey waves her free hand. "Forget him. Anyway, he'll be too busy with the battle to think of anything else. He lives for this stuff—or dies for it, actually."

"Dies for it?"

"Remember I said we argue about who has to die? One of the reasons the other guys put up with Luther is that he's always up for dying. Most reenactors don't like taking their turn, 'cause after you go down, there's nothing else to do. But Luther likes it because he can do a really impressive corpse. He gets all twisty and bloated somehow, and people take his picture like crazy. It's his thing."

I'm thinking about dying as a hobby when a phone buzzes. Tracey pulls out her cell. "Hi, Gram." Then she gets all serious looking. "Yeah, I did. Well, sorry, I didn't think you'd mind if we used it for…Well, like I said, sorry."

She's frowning. I guess I'm not the only grandchild in the world who messes up. She says, "We'll bring it back as soon—" A cannon goes off, and I almost jump out of my costume. "The what?" Tracey says. Another cannon roars. "Gram, I can't hear you. We're starting now. I've gotta go. Bye." She pockets her phone as another cannon fires, and another and another. Tracey steps back and hoists the camera into position. Basil jumps in front of me with a clapperboard.

"Sound," says Tracey.

"Speed," says Mark.

Pause. "Mark it," says Tracey.

Basil cracks the clapperboard. "Drift," he reminds me, and we're off.

NINETEEN

I tug on the rope and feel the cow start to move. I can't see it, but I can hear Laura Secord's bell clanking, and the rope is easy to pull. Somewhere behind me, I know, Tracey and Mark are following too. Just as I get a good glide going, I hear another phone buzz. Does everyone always call just as a battle is beginning? For a second I imagine a funny movie scene—everyone in an old-fashioned battle stopping to take calls on their cell phones. Then I notice that this phone sounds like mine. Then I remember I *have* mine.

Who's the only person that would call me now? Grandpa. This is not the time to answer. Anyway, they're not going to pause the fight while I take a call. Then, ahead of me, a ragged volley of musket fire drowns out my brain and my phone, and *BOOM*, a cannon drowns out everything.

I feel my heart start to pound. I know it's a pretend battle, but it doesn't seem like one. A veil of smoke drifts apart to show a line of redcoats. A couple of soldiers are already sprawled on the ground. I wonder if Luther has died yet. Then I think I hear Tracey. "Go right! To the right!" That will take me behind them. I tug on the rope. The clanking follows me. Ahead, a voice barks an order, and the redcoats aim their muskets. A sword catches the sun.

"FIRE!"

There's another terrible roar, and flame spits from musket barrels, and I shudder instead of glide as smoke and firecracker stink swallow us. Men cry out. A voice is shouting orders. I'm lost. Stumbling, I look for the trees. There's too much smoke, and the soldiers fire again, muzzle flashes through the haze, and then I see the trees, with a big dead one in the middle, as the sound of yelling gets louder and metal clashes.

Where are Tracey and Mark? Red and blue shadows flit through the gunpowder fog. I stumble again and jerk on the rope as I go down. I feel the cow stumble too. The guys in the costume must be even more confused than I am. My ears are ringing. Dimly, I can hear yelling. I struggle back up to my feet, tripping on the dress, dragging the cow guys after me. "C'mon," I shout to them. "We're almost at the trees." They're not much help. I stagger to the trees. From somewhere comes a thudding I can almost feel instead of hear. I spin and glimpse a horse running through the woods. I also see I'm not dragging the cow guys after me—I'm dragging the costume, with nobody in it. "BLEEP!" I yell, except I don't really yell *BLEEP*—I yell one of those words I'm not supposed to know. The exact second I do, something knocks me flat.

"BWOOF." I hit the ground hard. My hands slap the dirt, my glasses and the brim of the bonnet twist across my face, and my knee rams into something hard. For a microsecond, stunned, I wonder if something just punished me for swearing. I try to get up, and I'm knocked flat again. I hear panting and the clank of the bell, then a tearing noise. I roll over and tug the bonnet away from my face. A skinny man with a huge beard and black shades is kneeling, furiously trying to tear Laura Secord's cowbell away from the empty neck of the cow costume. He's wearing orange plaid shorts and a tiny straw hipster hat.

"Hey," I squawk, the strings of the bonnet choking me, "what are you doing?"

He doesn't even look up, and now, as I push my glasses into place, I see he has a knife in his hand. He's hacking at the costume with it. I scrabble back from him. Where are Tracey and Mark? Where are the cow guys? What's going on?

The man rips the head off the cow suit and takes the bell. Then he jumps up and starts to run, the knife in one hand and the bell in the other. As he does, something falls out of the bell.

"Bring that back!" I yell. "That's Laura Secord's!" This doesn't help. I roll again and grab whatever fell. It's a lump of something in duct tape. The guy is getting away through the trees. I do the only thing I can. I heave the lump at him.

Maybe I'm desperate, or maybe I've somehow learned from Bun's hatchet toss, but I hit the guy right between the shoulder blades. It's the best throw of my whole life. He yells, trips and goes down. His hat flies off into the weeds, and he lands on the bell.

I'm up and running at him before he hits the ground. It's not the fastest run of my life, but hey, running is tough in a pioneer dress and cargo shorts with stuff in the pockets. Then I remember that he has a knife. I stop running.

He groans and rolls over, still clutching the bell to his polo shirt. "Oh…man…" The hand holding the knife goes up to his jaw. "I think…I broke a tooth." He spits something out. "Awww, I did." He looks up at me. "You broke my tooth." The hand with the knife comes away from his face. So does part of his beard. Underneath it is a gigantic red sideburn.

"*Luther*?" I say. "What are you doing? Put the bell down, Luther, and just get out of here." I try to make my voice go flat and quiet like Grandpa's does when he gets mad. Apart from a squeak when I say *bell*, I think I do pretty good.

I guess Luther doesn't. He waves the knife. "Get lost," he snarls. I take a step back. Something bumps my knee and makes it hurt. I must have scraped it going down.

Luther lets go of the bell long enough to push at the fake beard. That makes things worse. Now it's hanging from one ear.

"C'mon, Luther," I coax. "Be careful with the bell. It's not farb."

"Yes, it is. You don't even know your own history. I'm getting rid of this garbage."

"Look, you won't get away with it. I'll tell everyone."

It's the wrong thing to say. Luther's eyes narrow, and the knife comes back up. "Really? Who's going to believe you? Huh?"

"Tracey and Mark have been following me, filming for their movie. They probably shot the whole thing." I'm hoping this is true. On the other hand, why aren't they here?

"Nice try," Luther sneers. "I followed you. They got lost in the smoke way back. It's just you and me, kid. Nobody'll believe you."

I look at the knife pointing at me. I remember the beef jerky on it. Would he use it for anything else? Maybe it's time to knock off the hero stuff. I take another step back. My knee gets bumped again. I realize what's been whacking it. "That's what you think," I say. I yank up the dress, grab my phone and aim it at him. I press the button and *click*, there's the camera sound. "I just took your picture," I say.

"What? Gimme that." He starts to get up.

"Don't move!" I shout. I've got the phone at arm's length, still pointed at him, like a gun, with my thumb up. It's probably not as impressive as a gun, but it freezes Luther. "If I press this button," I say, "the picture goes right to my grandpa. He's friends with Irene Steele, and you know what else he is? An explosives expert." Hey, Irene did say there were always fireworks when Grandpa was around. "Anything happens to me or that bell, when he sees this picture he'll come after you. He was in the real war, and he doesn't take prisoners."

Luther's shoulders sag, and he slumps back down to the ground. He calls me a name I'm not supposed to know, then tosses Laura Secord's bell into the weeds. It makes a muffled clank. "Take it." Wincing, he tries to reach back between his shoulder blades, then gives that up too. "You hit me."

"You hit *me*," I say. "We're even."

"Get lost."

"You get lost. I've got things to do." This is starting to sound like recess in grade two.

Wincing some more, Luther climbs to his feet. One of his boat shoes has come off. "Ow! I think I twisted my ankle." He grabs a sapling for support while he stuffs his bare foot back into the shoe. It's a very knobbly foot. Maybe 1812 boots do that to you. Now that he's standing up, I can see that his legs are as white and almost as skinny as mine. His orange plaid shorts are even bigger than my cargos. Luther puts the knife in a leather holder he pulls from a pocket, then bends over with a groan and gets his hat. "So go be a farb," he says over his shoulder. He limps away, rubbing his arms.

I wrestle the bonnet off. I see the clip-on microphone on the ground, dragging by its cord. I clip it back on, then walk over to Laura Secord's bell. The weeds are all mashed down where Luther fell. A big electrical cord snakes through them. I bet it's the same one I tripped over yesterday. I also see that the weeds are clusters of shiny leaves in threes—poison ivy. The bell is lying in poison ivy too. I lean in and pick it up using the bonnet.

As I step away carefully, a patch of silver-gray catches my eye. The lump of duct tape is not in poison ivy. I pick it up too. Inside the tape is the rusty caltrop, split in two. The halves are hollow. Inside one is a little chip like a computer memory card. How weird is that? The tape must have been holding the caltrop to the inside of the bell. I push the halves back together with the chip inside and fold the tape around them. I put the caltrop and the phone in my cargo pockets. Then I gather up the bonnet with the bell and what's left of the cow costume and start back the way I came, watching out for the old P.I.

TWENTY

I haven't gone far before I hear Tracey and Mark calling me. "Over here," I call back. We find each other a moment later. "Watch out for the poison ivy," I say.

"What happened to you?" Tracey exclaims. "Where are the cow guys? We lost you in the smoke; then Mark was getting this bizarre stuff on audio and then the sound conked out." She looks at the cow costume, and her eyes widen. "My god. Were you in a fight?"

"I lost the cow guys. I dunno where. Then Luther tried to steal the bell."

"*Whaat?* Oh, Spencer, I'm so sorry. I never thought in a million years—"

"It's okay," I say. "I took care of it." Although now that I've taken care of it, I'm feeling a little trembly. A lot trembly, actually. "Can you guys carry some of this? Careful—the bell has poison ivy on it. The dress might too. I think I have to sit down for a sec."

We come out of the trees by a picnic bench. I sit down and wait for the trembling to stop. Mark takes back the mic and battery pack. I wriggle carefully out of the dress. Around us, the battle appears to be over. Tourists are talking with reenactors, who are all alive again. Fiddle music drifts our way instead of gun smoke. I say to Tracey, "Luther said the bell was farb."

She lifts the bonnet and angles the bell so I can see inside. Just below some sticky bits left by the duct tape, it's stamped *MADE IN CHINA*. I look up at Tracey. She nods. "Luther's right.

Maybe they didn't cover it in history class, Spencer. Laura Secord really did walk twenty miles and warn the British, but she went by herself. No cow, and she didn't walk barefoot either. That would have been silly."

"Then why does your gram say she did?"

"Gram says history is in facts, but truth is in stories. I think she wants everyone to understand what a brave thing Laura Secord did and how everybody underestimated women." She looks at me. "They still do. Luther calls me a farb for acting the part of a soldier. I bet he would have thought twice about stealing the bell if you hadn't been dressed like a girl."

I think about that. I don't know if my stick legs in monster cargo shorts are going to scare anybody off, except maybe beavers looking for a bigger meal. Then again, Luther wasn't exactly the Mighty Hulk either.

Beside us, Mark's phone chimes. I remember mine buzzing as the battle started. I dig it out and check. Nobody called, which is a relief, now that I think of it. So whose phone did I hear? The cow's? That gives me another silly movie scene: cows in a field taking calls. Maybe I'm losing it.

"You feeling better?" Mark looks up from his phone. "We really need to get back to base and rethink. We're running out of time."

We stand up. "Did I do bad?" I ask.

"No, we did. We got some footage of you before we got separated, but not enough. And we've lost our cow guys, and the cow suit is kaput anyway, *and* Stef got hurt and can't walk around the site."

"How did she get hurt?" Tracey hoists the camera.

"The cow kicked her. So…"

They both look at me. I shake my head. "Sorry. My grandpa is taking us to brunch. And you told me *I* could film."

Tracey sighs. "You're right. It wouldn't work anyway. I mean, look at the costume."

She's right. The pioneer dress is smeared with dirt and plant stains. Lace hangs from one cuff, and the torn sash is dangling by a thread. The bonnet is just as bad, the brim all crushed. "Sorry," I say again.

"Hey," Mark says as we gather everything up, "you did your best. We'll improvise something. It's part of film."

Tracey nods. "You can help, but first we'll have to figure out what to film. Following Laura was going to tie it all together."

We follow the fiddle music back across the meadow. I've heard a lot of fiddle music this weekend, and I've learned something: I don't like it. It does give me an idea though. "Instead of following Laura Secord, why don't you follow Ken the fiddle guy around? He goes everywhere, and I sure don't think he's vegan."

"Heeey," says Mark. "Fiddle soundtrack." I shudder a little.

Tracey says, "Spencer, one day you'll be a director. We've got to talk to the others and check with Ken. Can you take the bell back? Gram will need it. She'll have to do her first talk soon. And tell her sorry, okay?"

TWENTY-ONE

I lug the cowbell back to the cabin. Lying in the bonnet, it doesn't clank. This is a good thing, as the clanking was getting on my nerves. It was almost as bad as the fiddle music.

Irene Steele has her spinning wheel set up on the porch again, and she's back in costume. Grandpa is standing near the cow, wearing his beret and aviator sunglasses, hands in the pockets of his chinos. He nods at it as I trudge up. "I wouldn't get too close, Spence. She kicked somebody a while ago."

"I heard," I say. "I'd have thought cows would like vegans."

Grandpa laughs. "How was the filming?" he asks as we walk over to Irene.

"Things got weird," I say. "But I get to do some more later."

"Weird?" Grandpa takes off his sunglasses. "How did it get weird?" Before I can answer, Irene is booming, "Spencer! And my bell! In the nick of time too—I shall be starting soon."

I hand over the bonnet. "The bell's got poison ivy on it. Clean it off before you touch it," I say loudly. "Tracey says sorry. She didn't think you'd mind."

"How did it get weird, Spence?" Grandpa repeats.

I don't answer because I'm watching Irene's hand sneaking up into the bell, even after I warned her not to touch it. How deaf *is* she? Whatever. It's her problem. But that reminds me of something, and I dig in my pocket. "Oh yeah. This fell out of it." I'm looking down, forgetting to be loud, but her head snaps toward me anyway.

"My caltrop!" she exclaims. "But of course."

It's Grandpa's turn for a head snap. He stares at both of us. Irene turns a little pink. "I put it in the bell for safekeeping. One treasure with another, and both dear to my heart."

"I didn't know the bell was fake," I blurt. "Luther tried to take it, and the caltrop fell out, so I hit him with it."

"*What*?" Now they're both staring.

I babble on. "I told you things got weird. Luther was mad about farb stuff. That's why I was trying to follow him last night. He said he was going to do something, but I didn't know what."

Grandpa looks at Irene. "Is Luther in the business?"

"Import/export?" I say. "No, he's a dentist."

There's a silence as they look at each other. Then Irene says, "Exactly. He's an over-eager young man with too much whisker and too little brain."

Grandpa nods. "Fair enough. I wouldn't want our caltrop idea getting stolen."

"Never fear, darling man." The caltrop disappears into the folds of her dress, and she's all smiles again. "Our business shall remain ours. As always. Now shoo, both of you. I have to prepare for my first talk. Spencer, a million thanks. I shall clean the bell immediately. Do come by later, both of you, and bring Bernard. TTFN." She stands and bustles into the cabin.

Grandpa and I step off the porch and into the sunlight. "She's quite a gal," he says, putting his aviator glasses back on. "I hate to think of her losing a step, but Lord knows we all get older. I thought she'd care for my little gift more than that."

"Grandpa," I say as we amble off, "I think the caltrop was a fake too."

"Why do you say that, Spence?" Grandpa's hands are in his pockets again. He's looking at everything but me.

"Well, when I hit Luther with it, it broke in two. It was hollow and there was, like, a little memory card inside it."

"Ahhhhh. Yes," Grandpa says. "I was teasing Irene about it being the real thing. She understood. The card has all the product and manufacturing specs for making the souvenirs. That's really why it was valuable. In our line of work, you always want your pitch package to stand out."

"I thought you were retired."

"Well, really I am, Spence, but I like to keep my hand in every once in a while, just for the fun of it. Call it a hobby. Keeps me young, like my grandsons do. And who knows? Irene and I might make a last little killing in our golden years." He starts to walk again. I follow. "Tell me, Spence, exactly how did you deal with this Luther character?"

I tell Grandpa how Luther tackled me and grabbed the bell and how I hit him with the caltrop.

Grandpa whistles. "Good for you. Damn risky, though, when he had a knife." He turns to me and takes his glasses off again. "I remember my wartime training. How did you take him?"

I figure now is the time. It's easier than lying anyway. I get out my cell phone. Grandpa's eyes widen, then narrow, but he doesn't say anything. I punch up the photo of Luther. "I told him I'd text this picture to you right then if he didn't drop everything and take off."

Grandpa blows out a breath, then nods and smiles at me. "Great play, Spence. Gutsy." Then he cocks an eyebrow and says slowly, "It's a good thing you had your cell phone."

"Yeah," I say. "It probably was."

Grandpa wraps an arm around my shoulders and gives me a hug. "Spence, do me a favor and send me that picture anyway. I want it for a souvenir." I punch the buttons. A moment later I hear Grandpa's cell phone ding.

"Thanks, bud. And one other favor. Let's not tell your parents—especially your mom—

everything we did this weekend, okay? Let's just keep some of this between you and me and Bernard."

It sounds good to me. In fact, it sounds way better than the fiddle music I hear coming closer. I turn and see Ken the fiddler strolling toward us. Tourists are gathering. Basil and Mark are walking backward in front of him with the camera and microphone. Tracey has the clapperboard. "Cut," Basil says.

Tracey comes over to us. "Ken's going to fiddle up a crowd for Gram." To me, she says, "How'd it go?"

"All good," I say. "Your gram isn't mad."

"Excellent. Thanks, Spencer."

"That's okay. Hey, can I film?" I have a feeling this is my last chance. Tracey goes to talk to Basil and Mark, then waves me over. "Go for it," Basil says.

Grandpa steps back. The camera settles on my shoulder. I check the eyepiece. This time it's clean. I settle my glasses. Basil plants the microphone boom near Ken but out of camera range. Tracey sets up with the clapperboard. I do a test focus. Ken swims into view, grinning as he saws away. Tracey steps in front of him. The clapperboard is marked *B 13 / 1*.

"Sound," I say.

"Speed," says Mark.

"Mark it."

Crack goes the clapperboard. Tracey steps out of the way. I keep the camera on Ken. People around him are swaying to the music. Some start to clap in time. Ken starts to stroll, and I follow. He's easing the people to where Irene Steele will talk. I catch a flash of Grandpa's beret, I think, in the background and then a patch of baby blue, the exact shade of a *BREAD* T-shirt from the 1970s. I sure hope it's Bunny. All at once, I'm starving. It's time for brunch.

ACKNOWLEDGMENTS

Tracing the threads of a story back can drive you crazy, but it's always worth doing, partly to remind you of the odd kinds of things that get your imagination going (the ridiculous cowbell sitting on the hearth at our summer cottage comes to mind) and partly to remind you how many people you should thank.

First off then, thanks to the Seveners (hey, Group of Seven is taken) for diving back in with a new twist to our collective saga of the McLeans. And hats off to Andrew and all at Orca for keeping the pool open for us.

Thanks especially to Richard Scrimger for being such a good sport and willing participant in closely linking our stories of Spencer and Bunny. Kicking ideas around with Richard and making things work always means the fun far outweighs the frustration when books are being cooked.

Thanks also to Rob Quartly, who patiently answered my questions about low-budget filming, and Ken Ramsden, trad musician *par excellence,* who is no stranger to the heritage reenactment scene.

My interest in the War of 1812 fittingly stretches back to one of my own grandpas, the late W.J. Stewart, who was instrumental in the preservation and restoration of Toronto's Fort York. You can find a plaque about him there if you visit the fort—something that's well worth doing, by the way.

My interest in reenactors began with a wonderful nonfiction book by Tony Horwitz, *Confederates in the Attic,* which, among other things, delves into the world of Civil War reenactors in the United States and introduced me to *farb* and *hardcore*. I'll confess right away that most of what I wrote about 1812 reenactors springs from my own imagination and the Horwitz book. My sincere apologies to actual 1812 reenactors if I've gotten things wrong. I'm sure you'll let me know.

Speaking of letting me—and us—know, thanks also to all the readers and supporters of Seven (the series) and the Seven Sequels. Your enthusiasm got us here.

Finally, as always, my thanks to Margaret and Will for love and good suggestions.

TED STAUNTON is the prize-winning author of many books for young people, from long-time picture book favorite *Puddleman* to the young-adult novel *Who I'm Not*. His novels *Jump Cut* and *Coda* are part of the popular Seven (the series) and Seven Sequels. Over the years he's also performed and led workshops everywhere from Inuvik to Addis Ababa. When not writing, Ted plays music in the Maple Leaf Champions Jug Band. Born very young, Ted is now older and lives with his family in Port Hope, Ontario. *Speed* is the prequel to *Jump Cut*, Ted's novel in Seven (the series).

THE SEVEN PREQUELS

HOW IT ALL BEGAN...
7 GRANDSONS
7 JOURNEYS
7 AUTHORS
7 ASTOUNDING PREQUELS

The seven grandsons from the bestselling **Seven (the series)** and **The Seven Sequels** return in **The Seven Prequels**, along with their daredevil grandfather, David McLean

JUNGLE LAND
ERIC WALTERS

9781459811492 pb
9781459811508 pdf
9781459811515 epub

THE MISSING SKULL
JOHN WILSON

9781459811584 pb
9781459811591 pdf
9781459811607 epub

TED STAUNTON
SPEED

9781459811614 pb
9781459811621 pdf
9781459811638 epub

RICHARD SCRIMGER
WEERDEST DAY EVER!

9781459811553 pb
9781459811560 pdf
9781459811577 epub

READ ONE. READ THEM ALL.
YOU CHOOSE THE ORDER

NORAH McCLINTOCK
SLIDE

9781459811676 pb
9781459811683 pdf
9781459811690 epub

SIGMUND BROUWER
BARRA CUDA

9781459811522 pb
9781459811539 pdf
9781459811546 epub

SEPARATED
SHANE PEACOCK

9781459811645 pb
9781459811652 pdf
9781459811669 epub

9781459811706 pb
9781459811713 pdf
9781459811720 epub

www.thesevenprequels.com

THE SEVEN SERIES
7 GRANDSONS
7 JOURNEYS
7 AUTHORS
1 AMAZING SERIES
ERIC WALTERS
BETWEEN HEAVEN AND EARTH
9781554699414 pb
9781554699421 pdf
9781554699438 epub
JOHN WILSON
LOST CAUSE
9781554699445 pb
9781554699452 pdf
9781554699469 epub
TED STAUNTON
JUMP CUT
9781554699476 pb
9781554699483 pdf
9781554699490 epub
RICHARD SCRIMGER
INK ME
9781459800168 pb
9781459800175 pdf
9781459800182 epub
CLOSE TO THE HEEL
9781554699506 pb
9781554699513 pdf
9781554699520 epub
SIGMUND BROUWER
DEVIL'S PASS
9781554699384 pb
9781554699391 pdf
9781554699407 epub
SHANE PEACOCK
LAST MESSAGE
9781554699353 pb
9781554699360 pdf
9781554699377 epub
SEVEN AMAZING ADVENTURES
7 AUTHORS 7 STORIES
9781459814295 pb
9781459802711 pdf
9781459802728 epub
"Richly detailed and satisfying."
-Kirkus Reviews
Available as audio!
www.seventheseries.com

THE SEVEN SEQUELS

7 GRANDSONS
7 NEW MISSIONS
7 AUTHORS
7 EXTRAORDINARY SEQUELS

Available as audio!

ERIC WALTERS
SLEEPER
9781459805439 pb
9781459805446 pdf
9781459805453 epub

JOHN WILSON
BROKEN ARROW
9781459805408 pb
9781459805415 pdf
9781459805422 epub

TED STAUNTON
CODA
9781459805491 pb
9781459805507 pdf
9781459805514 epub

RICHARD SCRIMGER
THE WOLF AND ME
9781459805316 pb
9781459805323 pdf
9781459805330 epub

SHANE PEACOCK
DOUBLE YOU
9781459805347 pb
9781459805354 pdf
9781459805361 epub

NORAH McCLINTOCK
FROM THE DEAD
9781459805378 pb
9781459805385 pdf
9781459805392 epub

SIGMUND BROUWER
TIN SOLDIER
9781459805460 pb
9781459805477 pdf
9781459805484 epub

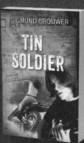

7 AUTHORS 7 STORIES

9781459814301 pb
9781459808236 pdf
9781459808270 epub

www.thesevensequels.com

SEE WHERE SPENCER GOES NEXT IN
AN EXCERPT FROM **JUMP CUT**
FROM SEVEN (THE SERIES).

"TWO SHOT"
BY SPENCER O'TOOLE

FADE IN:

EXT.—A COUNTRY ROAD—LONG SHOT, FROM ABOVE—DAY

A red Miata, top down, zooms along.

CLOSE—UP—SPENCER

SPENCER (Colin Farrell?) is behind the wheel. His
hair blows in the wind. He's all in black with cool
black shades. His chiseled face has a three-day beard.

EXT.—GATES OF HUGE MANSION—LONG SHOT, FROM
ABOVE—DAY

Miata turns in at gates of a huge mansion.

EXT.—STEPS OF MANSION—TRACKING SHOT FOLLOWS FROM BEHIND SPENCER—DAY
SPENCER strides up steps to mansion. Door opens. BUTLER nods.

INT.—MANSION HALLWAY—DAY
SPENCER walks down elegant hallway to giant doors. He opens them.

INT.—MANSION LIBRARY—WIDE SHOT (SPENCER'S POINT OF VIEW)—DAY
Two of Spencer's cousins, COUSIN DJ and COUSIN STEVE, are arm wrestling while playing chess. COUSIN ADAM flicks knives into a target across the room. COUSIN WEBB hangs upside down, texting. Spencer's brother BUNNY is on the couch, playing with a tiger. BUNNY looks at SPENCER and nods. The LAWYER sits at a big desk.

MEDIUM SHOT—LAWYER AT DESK
                    LAWYER
    Spencer. Good, we can get started. Gentlemen…

WIDE SHOT—GROUP AROUND DESK
All sit around desk in leather chairs.

                    SPENCER
Sorry I'm late.

                    COUSIN DJ
                (buttoning sleeve)
CIA again?

                    SPENCER
MI6.

                    COUSIN ADAM
              (putting knives in pockets)
They always call me when I'm making dinner.

                    BUNNY
                (stroking tiger)
It's nice to be wanted.

                    LAWYER
Ahem. Now then. Gentlemen, your grandfather's
will is a curious affair. But then, he was a curious
man.

All look up at painting of Grandpa in a massive,
ornate gold frame.

PAN TO:

CLOSE—UP—PAINTING OF GRANDPA

GRANDPA is wearing a cool leather flying jacket and a black beret. He's holding a Colt .45 and a compass.

LAWYER (OFF SCREEN)

Perhaps I should let him explain…

SPECIAL EFFECTS:

Picture turns misty and swirls into a hologram. Pixels resolve into a 3-D GRANDPA. He's dressed all in black and now he's got a glass of whiskey and a cigar.

GRANDPA

Boys—sorry, men. I have a final mission for each of you.